PRAISE FOR RACHEL VAN DYKEN

"*The Consequence of Loving Colton* is a must-read friends-to-lovers story that's as passionate and sexy as it is hilarious!"
——Melissa Foster, *New York Times* bestselling author

"Just when you think Van Dyken can't possibly get any better, she goes and delivers *The Consequence of Loving Colton*. Full of longing and breathless moments, this is what romance is about."
——Lauren Layne, *USA Today* bestselling author

"The tension between Milo and Colton made this story impossible to put down. Quick, sexy, witty—easily one of my favorite books from Rachel Van Dyken."
——R. S. Grey, *USA Today* bestselling author

"Hot, funny . . . will leave you wishing you could get marked by one of the immortals!"
——Molly McAdams, *New York Times* bestselling author, on *The Dark Ones*

"Laugh-out-loud fun! Rachel Van Dyken is on my auto-buy list."
——Jill Shalvis, *New York Times* bestselling author, on *The Wager*

"*The Dare* is a laugh-out-loud read that I could not put down. Brilliant. Just brilliant."
——Cathryn Fox, *New York Times* bestselling author

Finding Him

ALSO BY #1 *NEW YORK TIMES* BESTSELLING
AUTHOR
RACHEL VAN DYKEN

Covet

Stealing Her

Red Card

Risky Play
Kickin' It

Liars, Inc.

Dirty Exes
Dangerous Exes

The Players Game Series

Fraternize
Infraction

The Consequence Series

The Consequence of Loving
Colton
The Consequence of Revenge
The Consequence of Seduction
The Consequence of Rejection

The Wingmen Inc. Series

The Matchmaker's Playbook

The Matchmaker's
Replacement

Curious Liaisons Series

Cheater
Cheater's Regret

The Bet Series

The Bet
The Wager
The Dare

The Ruin Series

Ruin
Toxic
Fearless
Shame

The Eagle Elite Series

Elite
Elect
Enamor
Entice
Elicit
Bang Bang

Enforce
Ember
Elude
Empire

The Seaside Series

Tear
Pull
Shatter
Forever
Fall
Eternal
Strung
Capture

The Renwick House Series

The Ugly Duckling Debutante
The Seduction of Sebastian St. James
An Unlikely Alliance
The Redemption of Lord Rawlings
The Devil Duke Takes a Bride

The London Fairy Tales Series

Upon a Midnight Dream
Whispered Music
The Wolf's Pursuit
When Ash Falls

The Seasons of Paleo Series

Savage Winter
Feral Spring

The Wallflower Series (with Leah Sanders)

Waltzing with the Wallflower
Beguiling Bridget
Taming Wilde

The Dark Ones Saga

The Dark Ones
Untouchable Darkness
Dark Surrender

Stand-Alones

Hurt: A Collection (with Kristin Vayden and Elyse Faber)
Rip
Compromising Kessen
Every Girl Does It
The Parting Gift (with Leah Sanders)
Divine Uprising

Finding Him

RACHEL VAN DYKEN

SKYSCAPE

꘡ꓲꓲ꘡ SKYSCAPE

Text copyright © 2020 by Rachel Van Dyken
All rights reserved.

Published by Skyscape, New York

www.apub.com

Amazon, the Amazon logo, and Skyscape are trademarks of Amazon.com, Inc., or its affiliates.

ISBN-13: 9781542020886
ISBN-10: 1542020883

Cover design by Letitia Hasser

Cover photography by Lauren Perry

Printed in the United States of America

Finding Him

Chapter One

JULIAN

They say you never come back from death the same. I was evidence of that. Everything felt foreign, like I wasn't supposed to be in my own body, like something had altered my soul while I was sleeping and when it returned, it didn't quite fit in the body that woke up.

I snorted into my whiskey as the people around me talked in hushed voices like they were afraid my mom was going to jolt awake in the casket if they were too loud.

She was dead.

Dead.

I'd just seen her a week ago at the hospital; she'd been suffering with gastroparesis, a disease that made it impossible to digest food and sometimes even water. She'd been doing so well, and then one minor infection sent her into a downward spiral that even the best doctors money could buy couldn't fix. Couldn't help. Couldn't save.

An infection. Like a paper cut that gets ugly and red and refuses to go away, that's why she lost her life, not even the fucking disease but a side effect.

It was like she knew something was wrong. Right before she died, she'd made me promise to reconcile fully with the very twin brother who had stolen my life.

While I was in a coma.

How's that for a blockbuster movie?

And that ridiculously beautiful and intelligent woman had told me she loved me and made me say it—made me promise to try to be the bigger person—out loud. It was the last time I saw her, the last time I held her hand.

Her hands were cold now.

Placed at her sides perfectly, her makeup flawless, her dark silky hair arranged around her head like she was merely sleeping and waiting for her prince to rescue her, though we all knew the ugly truth. My father had been more dragon than prince, and the fact that she made it through their marriage unscathed was a miracle. He thought money meant he didn't have to suffer consequences and that love could be bought. He had no idea that the price would always be something he could never afford.

"How are you holding up?" My brother Bridge's voice interrupted my morose thoughts and intense concentration in the direction of the room that held our mother's body.

I didn't want a viewing.

Neither did Bridge.

But it was never just about us.

It was about our family name.

About what our father would also want, even though he no longer controlled Tennyson Financial, the largest financial corporation in the US. Even though he divorced our mother and cast her aside when we were teenagers, splitting my brother and me up in the process. I remained with my father, while Bridge lived with our mother.

But today, my father wanted the world to see the Tennyson men gather in strength, and I'd like to think that the bastard even suffered a bit of a broken heart at the sight of the love of his life without breath in her lungs and warmth on her skin.

The old Julian would have said he deserved it.

The Julian that woke up from that coma couldn't even look in the direction of the casket without tearing up and wanting to throw glassware all over the mansion.

"Fine." My voice was clipped, forced. "I'm fine, you?" I took another slow sip, my jaw clenched as Bridge stared me down.

We were identical twins.

He was a bit broader than I was, but now that I'd taken up lifting in order to work out the rage I had over the fact that he'd stolen my fiancée, it was even harder to tell us apart.

"Liar." He tilted the bottle of Jack into my glass. I let him, because I wasn't numb yet, because it hurt, because I had nobody to talk to.

Because I couldn't talk to him, not when I was still so angry at him.

It had been four months, and I still couldn't look at Izzy, who was now his wife. Because then I'd see the pity in her eyes, the sadness, the need for me to forgive her so she could get rid of her own guilt.

"Yeah, well, I'm a Tennyson." I lifted the glass to my lips. "What else you got?"

"You've been distracted lately." He pointed out the obvious, making my teeth clench. I needed him to be hateful, not caring, so I could continue hating him.

I scowled. "Can we not do this? Not only is the place crawling with media, but I don't need another lecture from my big brother on how to run my own company."

"That's not what this is about." He lowered his voice. "This is about you running yourself ragged, showing up to work looking like you haven't slept in years, dark circles under your eyes, cracked knuckles like the punching bag you spar with was pissing you off too much, the constant bouts of shouting I hear coming from your office when your secretary forgets to remove a staple before you shred something."

I rolled my eyes. "She has one job."

"This isn't you."

"Bullshit, this is the me you're going to get—"

"I met with the board."

This time I looked up into his green eyes, my all-too-familiar rage building like a pulse at my temples. He wouldn't. He didn't. Betrayal wrapped around my neck like a chokehold. "You did what?"

"The board, they're worried you're losing your grip, they wanted to see if I could force you to take a quick vacation."

I snorted out a bitter laugh. "I was in a coma for four weeks. Thanks, but I already took enough time off."

"You know what I mean."

"No, I don't." I jutted my jaw out, as if that would make me taller, and stood chest to chest with him.

"Guys." Izzy was suddenly at our sides. Her hand was on my shoulder, and I hated that I missed the way she used to touch me. I'd lost her the minute I brought her into this family when I thought I could balance my need for my father's approval with her love.

I had lost everything.

Everything.

My body swayed with exhaustion as she locked eyes with me and said, "Not here, not today."

"Tell him that." I gritted my teeth and glared at my brother.

Bridge shook his head like he was disappointed in me, again. I couldn't take it, I wanted to strangle him, to scream, to run headfirst into the nearest cement wall and just let it all disappear.

Maybe then I'd feel something.

Maybe something would knock sense into me.

"Jules." Izzy cupped my face with her hands. I clenched my jaw and drew back a few inches. Her touch was almost painful, because it was no longer just for me.

And now, she only had eyes for my brother.

Now she was pregnant with his child.

Now my life, the life I had planned with her, was as dead as the mother I never got enough time with.

My resolve was cracking.

My anger snapped into a downward spiral of sadness that had me wanting to run in the opposite direction so she didn't see the break in my defenses.

"Take the vacation," she whispered, her eyes full of unshed tears. "You can't go on like this."

"I can," I lied, wanting more than anything to look away from her perfect mouth, and the way it pressed into a firm, disapproving line that reminded me of all the reasons I was never good enough for her, and all the reasons my brother was.

"No." Her voice was soft, and then a solitary tear ran down her cheek, dripping onto the hardwood floor in slow motion. That tear was for me, it was for us, it was a tear that said so much more than words ever would.

Sometimes I hated myself.

Some days I hated her more.

Bridge looked ready to pummel me, probably because his wife was crying and I was the reason.

I hung my head, breaking eye contact. "Will three weeks get you guys off my case?"

"Yes." Bridge breathed a sigh of relief. "I'll tell the board, they'll be thrilled you're actually taking the mental health days."

I nodded, dumbly wondering what I was going to do alone in my new apartment for three weeks, when Bridge pulled something out of his pocket and handed it to me.

It was an old Polaroid of us at the cabin in Vermont. Our dad had had the place remodeled a few years back to make it look more modern, but a lot of the furniture was still the same, right along with the memories of my mom taking us sledding, making chili, and laughing late into the night around the campfire that we'd proudly built just for her. Our cabin was our escape from it all—Dad always cut his time there short and would often make excuses about having to go back to the city.

And we were always so thankful that he was gone. Once he left, our time there felt almost magical. The cabin was our own personal Disneyland, the happiest place on earth.

Some of my best memories were made there with my mom and Bridge.

It hurt so much to stare at the photo of Mom standing between my brother and me, her smile healthy, bright.

Tears stung my eyes. "The cabin?"

"You can do whatever you want." Bridge sighed and held the picture out for me to take it. "But they just got snow, and I know it would make Mom happy for one of her boys to be back there, celebrating, not mourning her death, but celebrating her life."

I cracked then.

With anger.

With sadness.

I took the picture and shoved him away. I didn't want his embrace, and I didn't want his love.

I just wanted to be alone.

The cabin . . .

Was the perfect place to start.

Chapter Two

KEATON

"Who is Keaton Westbrook?" I said it out loud about a dozen times as I gripped the steering wheel of the rental car and made my way down the dark road to the cabin I'd rented.

Was I just the daughter of some influential celebrity couple?

Was I just a college graduate trying to publish my very first book?

Was I a failure?

Was I still sad?

Depressed?

Was I even okay?

These are all the questions that pounded me on my way to my mini vacation to find myself, to see who I was without *him*.

Because I had defined my life up until that point as my parents' daughter. I was loved all over the US for my adorable celeb parents, and then I was nearly worshipped for my relationship with one of my fans.

A guy I'd met in the cancer wing at the hospital where I volunteered.

A guy who had changed my life forever.

A guy who became so much more than just a guy.

I went from barely living, not even appreciating my own oatmeal in the morning, to looking at every single moment as a gift. I went from selfie-taking influencer to appreciating small things, even when it rained.

God, he'd loved the rain.

You'd think it would depress him.

Not Noah.

He said rain meant that something new was coming, that fresh starts happened after a rain shower, and that we could consciously start anew.

So it made sense that it was raining as I drove to the cabin I'd rented for the month, didn't it?

It was a sign he was still with me.

Even though he never got his fresh start, his death brought me mine, along with my first publishing deal about our complicated relationship.

About our love.

Only I was so blinded by the pain of losing him, the pain I had thought I could pour into the pages, that I was stuck and on a deadline I couldn't force myself to meet.

Maybe because that meant we were finished, maybe because every time I thought of writing "The End," I couldn't breathe.

I was a year out of college.

I volunteered.

Sponsored ads for products on my Instagram and YouTube channels.

Had my own beauty line at Sephora.

And in between those projects, I had my laptop, and I still couldn't write the first chapter.

Because it made it true.

It made his death real.

I tried not to cry as I hit the accelerator and thought about his soft golden hair, the way it would stick up on all ends when I ran my fingers through it. Men in Hollywood would kill for that hair. Noah was too beautiful for words. Even when he started losing his hair, his eyebrows, even when he lost the ability to speak.

He was enough.

He would always be enough.

More than I would ever deserve.

I rubbed the tears on my cheek away as my GPS told me to take another right. I pulled into a long driveway and sighed in relief. Too much time in the car did that to me, it made me reflect.

It made me do exactly what I was supposed to be doing, except I should be writing those things down on paper, or at least typing them into the computer.

"You can do this." He'd winked and squeezed my hand. *"C'mon, K, tell me our story . . ."*

More tears filled my eyes until I could barely see the modern cabin in front of me. It was made up of huge floor-to-ceiling windows, had a wraparound deck, and was three stories. I knew the back would have an infinity pool that overlooked the lake and a dock I could sit at the end of.

It also had five bedrooms and three bathrooms.

This was where Noah had wanted to go for our honeymoon, a fact he mentioned when we were daydreaming about our future while waiting for more test results. I thought he was going to propose, thought it was a cute way to test the waters.

But he never did.

When I asked him why not, his smile was so sad my chest felt like someone was pressing a bulldozer against it.

"It's not fair, K." He tucked my hair behind my ears and kissed my nose. His face was pale, his lips a bit cracked as he licked them. "I'm not going to steal part of your future. You deserve to get asked by a guy with a clean slate, by a man who loves you more than life. Let me love you through death, let me do my job. Yours is to find someone who will deserve that smile."

"Noah—"

"Shhh." He pressed a finger to my lips. "No more tears, I want to look at the cabin again."

I let out a snort. "More like mansion in the woods. Whoever owns this is clearly loaded and would probably mob us the minute we came into the house or plant cameras somewhere and sell the pictures."

"Aw, is the little celebrity jealous of the cabin in the woods?" he teased with a wink and then pulled my phone away and kept scrolling. "Remember, don't focus on negativity." He paused. "Do me a favor and rent this place someday."

"I promise." My lips trembled.

He looked over at me and softly exhaled. "Don't cry, we all die someday, the only difference is you get more time than I did. Try not to be a jerk and waste it, beautiful."

"Okay, Noah." I killed the engine and grabbed my purse. "You win. I'm here. Now what?"

Chapter Three

It took me a solid two hours to get everything completely unpacked and into the master bedroom, with its ginormous empty king bed, flat-screen TV, and gorgeous stone-tiled bathroom. It even had a door that led to an outdoor shower. Showering outside while it snowed sounded so sexy and freeing.

And just like that, my little bubble popped.

He would have loved it here.

I was a beach sort of girl, but Noah? He loved the mountains, said they made him feel like there was something bigger in the universe, something majestic. It was why he wanted to honeymoon here in the first place. He'd laughed when I suggested Turks and Caicos.

It was our differences that made our relationship unique. I'd felt like a spoiled brat next to him; he'd brought out a part of me that I hadn't even realized needed fixing until he pointed it out. I was so consumed with myself, and then, after Noah, consumed with him, with life, with us.

I swallowed the lump in my throat as I pulled a gray hoodie over my T-shirt. I was already wearing black skinny jeans to which I added a pair of white snow boots as I tried to cart everything inside the cabin, including groceries. There was supposed to be a huge storm coming in, and I wanted to be prepared, right down to an emergency case of wine and two bottles of whiskey.

Alcohol served two purposes: it kept you warm out on the slopes and could disinfect anything and everything.

First aid and fun!

Though drinking by myself sounded more depressing than fun.

I grabbed a container of ground beef and put it in the sink to thaw while I unloaded the rest of the groceries. The good news was if the blizzard wasn't horrible, I'd be able to explore first thing in the morning, make some coffee, and maybe, just maybe, get some writing done.

As if conjuring itself into existence, my laptop made a noise alerting me to a text to my phone.

Mom: You safe?

I smiled at the screen. My dad was directing a movie, and my mom took time off so she could be with him. They were in some secret location in London.

Me: Oh good, I still have service.

Mom: Sarcasm? Are you being sarcastic right now?

I burst out laughing at my phone and shook my head as pieces of my honey-blonde hair fell down around my shoulders.

Me: Never.

Mom: Good . . .

Oh, sweet Lord, save me from the ellipsis.

Something sad always followed those three little dots.

It was her version of a *but*.

I waited.

And waited.

Finally, it came.

Mom: . . . I'm worried about you. You're just so sad all the time, and I know the news can be relentless. Thank God that whole fiasco with Tennyson Financial happened and finally took the heat off you. Small favors, you know? Just think about it, while you were able to mourn in semi-forced peace, those two boys were throwing punches at a wedding and planning a hostile takeover. Can you imagine?

I sighed, vaguely remembering the scandal. Apparently one of the chief officers was in a coma, his twin took his place at the company, and his then fiancée knew or didn't know? Regardless, the one woke up, the other apologized, and it was front-page news for a really long time. And after all that, the two brothers even voted out their own father and took over one of the biggest financial corporations in American history.

So naturally, that would take precedence over a Hollywood romance with its sad ending.

After all, nobody was interested in the way Noah and I ended. It wasn't happy, and people liked the happy ending. They wanted to root for the underdog; they didn't want him to die a painful death.

It was too realistic. Too close to home.

And people these days needed something that gave them hope, not made them realize how utterly sad life could actually be. The media firestorm happened during our relationship, followed by radio silence until I announced I was writing a book, and then my social media exploded to the point that the attention was almost scary.

Mom: Sorry, I said too much. Are you still there?

Me: Sorry, was just thinking. I'm unpacking, I'll call tomorrow, I'm safe, I'm fine, send a helicopter if you get worried, hah hah.

Mom: Don't tempt me.

Me: OMG Mom I'm twenty-four cut me some slack. Don't send Gene!

Gene Springsteen was a family friend who did a lot of stunt work and was known as Hollywood's young Chuck Norris. My mom had also been trying to set me up with him since Noah in order to cheer me up. I wasn't interested in anyone. And I couldn't imagine feeling anything for someone other than the man I buried.

Mom: Fine. I love you!

Me: I love you too.

I set my phone down and looked around what would be my home for the next month and realized in that moment that I hated the silence. I needed a TV on or something that would make me feel anything but as lonely as my heart reminded me I was.

How was I supposed to write our story? My story with Noah? When all I could focus on was the fact that I was there, living his dream, while he was in the cold hard ground.

Tears welled in my eyes.

"Goodbye is just that, a really good farewell," he wrote out with a shaky hand on the notepad I'd been forced to give him. His hand dropped the pen and reached for my cheek, then fell away lifeless against the white duvet.

I spent a lot of time watching him sleep wondering if he would wake up again and continue our conversations about death. I had imagined the end would look different, but when Noah died it was as if he realized it was time to go and, like a bird, took flight.

I swiped hot tears from my cheeks and turned toward the large living room windows just in time to see headlights drawing closer to the cabin through the snow that had started coming down like a freaking blizzard while I took my trip down memory lane.

Headlights?

Out here?

If it was Mom, I was going to kill her.

If it was Mom and Dad, I was going to lose it.

At least it wasn't a helicopter, which meant I was safe from Gene.

It was too dark to see anything but the headlights and the black of the car. I moved closer. Maybe the owners decided to check up on me? That had to be it.

Then again, no one mentioned that possibility when I put down my deposit.

A cold chill trickled down my spine when I realized how alone I was out here. I had cell service, but it wasn't like I carried a weapon on me; I was completely defenseless.

I ran back to the kitchen, my eyes darting around for something to grab that wasn't a mixing bowl or bottle of whiskey. I jerked a serrated steak knife free from the butcher block and turned toward the door. The cabin had an open floor plan for the living room and kitchen. I was at least twenty feet from the door as the sound of a key sliding through metal had my blood chilling even more. Then the knob turned as I hid my knife behind my back and had my free hand on my cell ready to call for help.

The door was shoved open.

I sucked in a sharp breath as a man made his way through carrying an expensive-looking camel-colored leather bag and another smaller suitcase.

His eyes roamed the room and landed on me.

The knife in my hand nearly clattered to the floor as I gaped.

Male. Perfection.

I hadn't noticed a man, any man, since Noah.

But this man demanded notice.

It was in the air around him, in the way his green calculating eyes took a person in, like he was measuring every single thing about those he encountered and deciding if they were worth his time—all within the span of one blink.

His hair was tousled to the right of his head, like he'd run his hands through it one too many times, and his jaw was so chiseled and his cold cheeks so handsomely ruddy that I almost looked away in embarrassment. Staring longer than a few seconds without speaking was creepy enough.

"Clever," he said after a long pause, his tone bored, as he dropped his bags on the floor in supreme irritation. "And no, I won't give you a story, so you better just leave."

"St-story," I repeated, trying to figure out if he was sane or not, as I gripped the knife like a lifeline. Ted Bundy was gorgeous too. *Remember Ted Bundy!* "What do you mean *story*?" I backed away slowly, waiting for the killer smile, or the comment about my looks that almost always started with "Do you model?" If he was a Ted Bundy, he'd hit on me, right? Make me feel safe?

"You're with the media?" His right eyebrow arched mockingly. "I mean you look like hell, what did you do? Drive all day just to get the scoop?" I almost argued with him. *I* looked like hell? *He* looked like he'd misused a blow dryer, not that it made him look bad, quite the opposite. "I didn't talk to anyone at the funeral and I'm not going to talk to anyone now. Fucking. Leave."

His harsh language jolted me and I glared. "I'm not the media, I'm a person, and I literally have no idea what you're talking about." Good one. "And I rented the house for one full month and paid ahead, so if anyone's *leaving*, it's you!"

His eyes narrowed into tiny, intimidating slits that told me he wasn't used to the word *no*. "Impossible."

"Possible!" I stood my ground. "I have confirmation and everything. I booked this place ahead of time, unlike you! What? Did the owner feel sorry for you and give you a key so you could run away from the media?"

His face paled.

I instantly felt guilty. I knew firsthand what it was like to feel like a big fish while all the sharks circled and waited for blood.

"Sorry." I swallowed and looked away from his thunderous expression. "That was uncalled for. Let me start over . . . I'm—"

"Don't care." He waved me off and walked toward me until he was nearly towering over my small frame. "I don't care who you are, you need to leave. I'm sorry for the inconvenience, and I'll pay you back in full if you give me your information."

"No." I squinted up at him. "Who the hell do you think you are? I'm not leaving! I booked this place! I need solitude, damn it!" This was not happening!

His scowl deepened. "Exactly." His grin was taunting, mean, and I didn't like it. He was beautiful before, but now he just looked cruel.

"Solitude does sound nice, that's why I drove my ass up here. Look, I'll give you triple what you paid."

I did the mental math. "Oh, so you're just going to whip out the trusty old checkbook and give me over a hundred thousand dollars?"

He didn't even flinch. Who was this guy? "Only a hundred thousand?"

"Huh?"

"Thought they rented it out for more than that these days, around three grand a night seems cheap."

My jaw dropped. Actually, it was incredibly expensive, but I loved the modern setup and it had a pool and a hot tub and was so close to the water you could throw a rock in it. I tried a new tactic. "Unless I can cash the check now, that's going to be a no. Why don't we just call the owner and let them explain since you seem to be having trouble with the concept of 'already rented out.'" I smiled politely even though on the inside I was seething.

His eyes trained on mine and then he reached into his back pocket and pulled out a cell phone. Someone answered immediately. "Yes, I'm going to need a hundred-twenty-thousand-dollar cashier's check made out to—"

I balled my fists. "Put your phone away!"

"Hold on . . . Your name?"

"Put it away!" I hissed.

He looked genuinely confused.

"I don't want your money!" I said through gritted teeth. "I want the cabin, all to myself, for thirty days so I can—" I felt the tears then, the tears of sadness, frustration, the tears I refused to shed at the funeral and ever since because it just made it more real and I was afraid if I started I wouldn't stop. Angry, angry tears. "I don't need it!"

One fell.

I brushed it away before he could see that he, a perfect stranger, had the ability to make me cry.

"Are you . . . seriously that upset over a cabin?" He laughed at that like I was an idiot. "You know, there's more to life than pretty things. There's a big old world out there with hurt and betrayal and humans who like to make others suffer. There's people dying of cancer, people curing it, people who don't know where their next fucking meal is coming from, and you're . . . crying?"

His rage was misdirected.

His fists clenched.

We were at a standstill.

"Don't pretend to know me," I whispered hoarsely. "I don't need your money, and unless you can find me someplace close that looks identical to this one, for the same price, I'm staying. You're gonna have to find a hotel or something, Mr. Moneybags."

"Moneybags?" He snorted.

I jerked my head to his suitcase. "Louis Vuitton suitcases, your sweater's cashmere, your jeans are Dsquared2, shoes Prada, I bet your hair gel costs more than most people's electric bill, and I'm pretty sure I just smelled a hint of Clive Christian. So yes, Moneybags."

He took a step toward me, cursed under his breath, and then reached for me just about the same time I held the knife between us and under his chin.

Self-defense and all.

He looked down at the knife, surprise written all over his face. "Do you even know how to use that thing?"

"Sure, I just shove it in and twist, right?" I smirked.

"You're a crazy person!" He didn't sound afraid, more impressed than anything.

"You're the crazy one! Showing up at night, demanding I leave when—"

I let out a little scream as the lights completely went out and found myself dropping the knife and grabbing his arm like it was the only thing that was going to keep us safe.

He didn't pull away.

Just dropped a few more curses that told me he'd rather be any-where than in the dark with me and my knife-wielding.

"I don't suppose"—I licked my dry lips—"that the owner just for-got to pay the electricity bill?"

"The storm." His voice sounded deeper in the dark, grittier, and then another whiff of his cologne caught me as he pulled out some-thing, his cell, and dialed another number. "Bridge, yeah, I'm here. Funny, though, someone else is too? At our cabin."

Oh no, no, no, no.

His cabin?

He was the owner?

Asshat of the year?

"She won't give me her name but she pointed a knife at my throat, so if I'm in the news again, remember, this is all your fault."

I scowled as my cheeks heated with embarrassment. "I didn't try to kill you."

"Yeah, that's her." He completely ignored me. "I'm not answering that. Look, the power just went out, and she booked it for one full month so I need to find a place, but the weather is shit. Have Kelsey find me a place to stay for the next few weeks that *isn't* occupied, will you? Either that or find a way to get this interloper the hell out."

"Still here," I muttered.

"Still not answering that."

What was he being asked?

"You're such a pain in the ass, Bridge. No, damn it. Now go be annoying elsewhere . . . I'm staying the night so you don't find my frozen body later. Bye."

He hung up. And turned to face me. The snow and all the floor-to-ceiling windows helped the lighting a bit.

He was too pretty to be so angry. The slant of his eyes was assessing as he looked down at the Italian marble floor then back to me, his full lips pressed into what looked like a judgmental smile. I gulped, waiting

19

for him to say something. I was close enough to feel his body heat; it pulsed in cadence with his anger, and it was all directed at me.

"I'm assuming a girl who knows how to wield a knife knows how to build a fire?"

I gave him a light shrug. "I mean I don't think I could survive *Naked and Afraid*, but I could manage a fire."

"Perfect." He grinned coldly. "Build a fire."

And then he was shoving past me.

"Wait! What are *you* going to do?" He moved toward the breakfast bar like . . . well, like he owned the place, which apparently he did. I was ready to remind him that I was a paying tenant and that the food and everything else was mine, but I was distracted by his confident swagger. Had he just been born with it? Or was it a learned habit?

"Me?" He gave me an incredulous look as he pulled out my whiskey and unscrewed the top. "I'm gonna drink. Better hurry, the firewood should be out front, but it's getting cold. I'd hate to see you freeze a finger off. How would you hold a knife then?"

"You're going to get drunk while I take care of our basic human needs?"

"Think of it this way . . ." He smirked. "If you don't build a fire, we're going to have to get naked and share body heat, and I highly doubt that would be your first choice, since you're already so fucking frigid."

I almost picked up the knife.

I almost threw it at his perfect face.

Instead, I took the high road, flipped him off, and went in search of my coat.

Well, at least he wasn't Ted Bundy.

Just a grumpy millionaire who forgot he'd rented out his cabin to someone who needed it more than he did.

Perfect.

Chapter Four

JULIAN

There was something vaguely familiar about her heart-shaped face . . . maybe it was the full lips? They were more pink than red, and seemed to turn up in a snarl every time I opened my mouth.

Who the hell was she? And why didn't my secretary make sure that the cabin wasn't rented? Then again, I'd been in such a hurry to get the hell out of the city it probably wouldn't have mattered. I wanted my cabin, I didn't care if someone else was in it. It was mine, and she didn't belong.

I tipped the whiskey back, reveling in the smooth burn as it hit the back of my throat. At least she knew her alcohol. I was in a foul mood, and finding some random stranger in the same cabin that my mom used to take us to when we were kids, before the divorce, just made it that much more invasive.

She was in my space.

Our space.

She was strutting around in our memories, sitting in places I remembered my mom sitting in.

I hated it.

And I hated her because of it.

She had no right.

The minute I was back in the city I was going to take this place off whatever rental site it was on, permanently. Strangers had no business in our lives.

I poured two shots of whiskey into my coffee cup and watched while the strange woman slammed the door behind her, only to come back minutes later without any firewood.

She stared me down.

I lifted my mug.

She looked like she wanted to lift a middle finger again and was barely restraining herself from doing so as she clenched her teeth and got out a terse "I can't find it."

"What?" I smirked tossing the rest of the whiskey back.

"Wood." She crossed her arms.

My eyebrows shot up to my hairline. "Oh?"

She let out a sigh and threw her hands up in the air. "I looked where you said to look, I used the flashlight on my phone, and everything is covered in snow."

"And you're still here because . . ."

"I need help," she said as she slowly eyed me up and down as if measuring to see if I was the sort of man who even knew how to light a match let alone build a fire. "Since you seem to own the place you should at least be able to look out the door and point, right? Or is that too difficult for your pea brain to manage?"

"Pea brain." I snorted out a laugh. "Nice. If I wasn't so intelligent and rich, I might actually be insulted. Then again, we aren't in middle school, so . . ."

Her eyes flashed with fury. She was on the shorter side, and her coat was puffy enough to hide every single curve I'd taken notice of the minute I opened the door.

Fact, her skin was flawless.

Fact, her hair was shiny even though it was pulled up into a knot on the top of her head.

Fact, most women were manipulative, so the second I took notice, I'd looked away, and well, the minute she'd opened up her mouth, I realized that finding her attractive wasn't going to be a problem. Finding a muzzle in this blizzard, however, would be.

I slowly stood, taking my time to stretch my legs after such a long car ride, lazily made my way toward the front door, then looked over my shoulder. "You coming or are you just going to wait until my back's fully turned before you stab me with the kitchen knife?"

"I'm not a murderer." She crossed her arms and stomped toward me, snow falling off her boots in a nice little trail that one of us would have to clean up later. "Just point and I'll go since you don't want to ruin your manicure."

I barked out a laugh. "Manicure, wow, impressive you even know what that is." I eyed her clenched hands and nodded. "Tell me, do you collect dirt in your fingernails as a hobby or is it just a fetish?" It was a lie; her fingernails were perfect, I just wanted a reaction.

She ground her teeth. Well that was my answer!

"Scientific experiments sound better. Maybe go with that. You're a scientist and every speck of dirt counts. I like it." If I wasn't careful, she really was going to grab the knife. I jerked open the door and pointed to the north side of the house. "It's against that wall. All you have to do is march in that direction, make sure you don't get mauled by a bear, and collect enough wood to make sure we don't freeze to death. Easy."

"Bear." She gulped. "As in, there's only one bear and you've seen it? Or that there could be a bear?"

"Sorry." I crossed my arms. "I meant bears, plural, but it's winter, and they should be hibernating, so unless you've rolled naked in Nutella you should be good to go."

"That's your example?" she nearly screeched. "Naked in Nutella?"

"I'm tired." I shrugged. "And conversing with you has officially taken up my quota of words for the day." I jerked my head toward the wood pile. "Go."

"Such a gentleman," she muttered, shoving past me out into the night. I could have sworn she stomped the entire way to the side of the building.

A small part of me felt guilty for making her go out in the cold, but it quickly dissipated when I remembered the reason I was there.

The reason I was facing the snow in the country instead of a light rain in the city.

Mom.

I swallowed the lump in my throat as a flash of her perfume hit me, the sound of her laughter after skiing and coming back to the house to roast marshmallows.

Whoever this stranger was.

She had no business stomping around my memories and facing me at my worst. I needed to grieve, to sit in silence and wonder how everything went so fucking sideways when all I'd ever wanted was to just make it out of my family alive.

Take the company from my father.

Reconcile with my brother.

See my mother.

It all came true.

But it was wrong, like an alternate universe. Instead of being a part of the story of riding into the sunset with my fiancée and cutting a check for my brother saving the day.

Bridge had done it, he'd been my fiancée's hero while I was just the cheating jackass who was forced to play a part in order to get what I wanted.

I was a Tennyson.

I knew how to manipulate.

I knew how to read people.

I knew how to get what I wanted.

Until a coma knocked me on my ass.

And my older-by-a-few-minutes brother swept in.

I wanted to let it go.

But the betrayal cut deep.

The knowledge that while I was sleeping, fighting for my life, his hands were on her, his mouth pressed against hers, his words breathing life into the corpse I'd left behind.

He'd fixed what I'd broken.

And selfishly, I didn't want to forgive him for that because it meant I was in the wrong, it meant that no matter what I was willing to sacrifice for my ambition, that it had been too much, because in the end it had been Izzy.

Our relationship had been smashed to pieces long before the coma, and I was the one holding the hammer.

I checked my watch and glanced at the dark shadow of the wall. She still wasn't back yet.

Seriously?

How long did it take to get wood?

I waited another two minutes before the feeling of panic started to set in. I was an ass, but I didn't want her to freeze to death, just to learn her lesson and hate me enough to want to leave midstorm.

I cringed.

Mom would slap me.

I quickly grabbed my coat from inside, then started the trudge toward the wall. When I rounded the corner, the infuriating strange woman was leaning against the wall with her tongue out as snowflakes fell against her face and melted onto her skin.

Another lifetime ago, I would have thought it erotic.

Maybe even mesmerizing.

But in that moment all I wanted to do was strangle her. "Dehydrated or just trying to be a pain in the ass?"

"Both." She didn't look at me. "It was a test. You passed—barely."

"A test?" I started grabbing firewood, ignoring the way she seemed to stare right through me. I ignored the prickling awareness across my skin.

"Yup." She popped the *p* and started a fresh stack in her own arms. "I figured a true gentleman would get worried and come outside to make sure I was still breathing, and a complete jackass from the city would just assume I died, which meant he could drink all my alcohol without any competition."

"There's a flaw in that logic." I grunted, picking up a few more pieces of firewood and turning to stare at her. "I'm an ass through and through, I was just a really cold ass. Had I found your frigid body lying in the snow, though, I would have at least said a quick prayer before putting a candy bar in your hand and waiting for the bears." I winked.

She looked ready to beat me with the firewood, only after making it pointy enough to impale me.

With a smirk, I started whistling and walked back toward the door. "Hurry up before I lock you out."

She stumbled behind me, cursing me to hell the entire way, and for some reason it made me smile.

Not just a forced smile.

But one that made my face almost hurt.

All because she mumbled under her breath that she was going to set me on fire while I slept.

"I'll be sure to sleep with one eye open, sweetheart," I muttered softly, earning another curse from her as she started piling the firewood next to the fireplace.

And when she looked up to give me another scathing look, I broke eye contact.

Pretty.

She was pretty.

Not that it mattered.

Because my heart might as well have been buried in that casket next to my mom's. God knows that's how my soul felt, like the dirt was trying to pull me under, trying to bury me along with my mother.

I was just as dead as she was.

And I had to wonder if maybe, maybe the world was better off without Julian Tennyson fully existing in it.

Chapter Five

KEATON

He was lucky I wasn't grabbing more sharp objects and pointing them in his direction. The fire roared from the living room, and every few minutes he would take a sip out of his coffee cup while he stared into the flames.

I'd managed to get a small fire started.

But I hadn't done it well, at least not well enough for the rich owner's approval. Within minutes of my blowing on the small flame, he was kneeling down next to me and lighting different pieces of newspaper, stuffing them under the kindling like a pro, and then giving me a look that basically said he was above me in intelligence in every single way that mattered.

That was an hour ago.

The snow hadn't let up.

I kept mentally praying for a miracle, ready to switch to whatever religion would get me out of this place, or better, get him out of my hair.

The silence was going to kill me.

And since the power was out, no TV, no Netflix, no anything.

Finally accepting my fate, I grabbed my laptop and sat cross-legged on the nice leather couch and opened up my writing program.

The cursor blinked at me from the empty page, waiting for the words that wouldn't come, words that I needed if I was going to actually turn in something worthwhile in the next month.

I closed my eyes despite the stranger in the room drinking heavily and silently fighting whatever demons he had, and I thought of Noah.

Ever smiling.

Always comforting.

Noah.

Where he had been warm, this rich stranger was cold.

Where he had been optimistic, this guy made me feel like he was seconds away from screaming that the sky was falling.

Why was I even comparing them?

I opened one eye and then the other. He was staring at me intently.

I could see the piercing green of his eyes from my spot on the couch, the fire helping illuminate his sculpted face. I wondered what he looked like when he was actually amused, when he didn't feel the need to talk down to a person he'd just met.

I refused to look away, assuming he would back down.

He didn't.

Instead, he lifted the coffee mug to his full mouth as a wicked grin curved his lips. "What's your name?"

"You won't need to know it since you're leaving in the morning," I said with all the enthusiasm of someone who just got a flu shot in the eye.

His blink was slow as he lowered the mug and set it on the coffee table in front of him. We were maybe five feet away from one another. For such a huge house, the living room was oddly inviting and warm, with the furniture strategically arranged to make the area cozy—a bit too cozy to spend with someone who viewed you as the help.

"I take it you haven't looked outside." His right brow shot up a bit, and then he sucked in his bottom lip and sighed. "This is what meteorologists call a blizzard. I'm just praying my car isn't buried in the morning, and since we're stuck together I'd at least like to know what name to give my family when they find my cold corpse buried beneath the snow."

I would not laugh.

He wasn't charming.

I swallowed a smile and tilted my head. "You planning on being even more insulting in the future? I mean you must, since you think I'm over here plotting your death."

He just shrugged. "I'm pretty sure my breathing annoys you."

"You didn't ask, you *told* me to build a fire, like I was some hired help, plus you tried to throw money at me when I wouldn't go away, so kind of annoyed yes, more disappointed in mankind than anything, though." I flashed a grin then glanced back down at my laptop.

Focus.

Honestly, he hadn't done anything horrible in the last hour, he'd even helped with the fire, but something about him rubbed me the wrong way, even his silence made me want to throw something.

He was ruining my solace.

And up until that point, I hadn't realized how badly I needed to just sit and think and be alone.

A person like me was never alone; constantly surrounded, whether by social media, photographers, or my parents' insane amount of staff. There was always someone. My parents were A-list celebrities, my mom an actress and my dad an award-winning director. Growing up in the limelight meant everyone was always willing to bend over backward for you—even if they hated you. When Noah died, the noise around me made the choking sensation in my throat worsen, because when people don't know what to say, they say they are sorry, and they ask if you're okay, and I didn't trust myself not to break down. Social media used to feel like an escape, and now it felt more like a dungeon because I couldn't grieve the way I knew I needed to, not in front of millions of people and not with someone asking me if I needed anything every few seconds. Every single time they tried to be nice, I had to fake a smile.

And I was fresh out of those.

I think I used my last one on him.

See? Selfish!

I typed "Noah." My fingers shook.

And then my laptop was slowly being shut. I moved my hands to keep from getting them caught and glared up at the guy responsible.

I had no choice but to scoot over as he sat down on the couch next to me, his whiskey cup in his hand. "I'm Julian."

"I didn't ask."

"Tennyson," he finished.

And I couldn't not react.

Tennyson?

The Julian Tennyson?

The one who was in the coma and all over the news? His brother and his former fiancée were expecting a child. It was like a bad soap opera.

What were the odds?

"If you ask me if I'm that Julian, the one who was in a coma, I'll probably set myself on fire to get a head start on my murder. Consider yourself warned."

I sighed, pulling my laptop to my chest. "I don't have to ask what I already know."

He stared ahead into the flames. "Normal people can't afford this place."

It wasn't a question, more of a statement than anything.

I said nothing and let him keep talking.

"Your boots are Wyn, one of the hardest brands to get ahold of during Fall Fashion Week, you have lip injections, just enough to make your upper look a bit bigger than your lower, your hair's tinted, not dyed, giving it the appearance that the color is natural when it's not. Your fingernails aren't painted but manicured to the point that I doubt you even know what a callus feels like. You smell like Gucci, and I already saw the GG Marmont bag in the corner."

I gaped up at him.

"You don't need to tell me your name, princess. I know exactly your type, I've been around it all my life, a name changes nothing." He stood and called over his shoulder, "Good night."

I felt scolded as I watched him disappear down the hall, and then I felt something I hadn't felt in a really long time.

Shame.

Like I had something to hide from him, something that made him better than me. How dare he make me feel that way!

He didn't know me.

I flipped open my laptop, ready to pour out my soul, my frustration, and ended up doing nothing but staring at pictures of Noah and me, and swiping the tears that leaked onto my cheeks.

I was miserable.

Stuck with Julian Tennyson, one of the richest men alive.

And wouldn't you know, *People* magazine's most sought-after bachelor.

And all I wanted to do was march into his room and tell him he was wrong.

But I had no fight left in me.

And I was afraid the minute I opened my mouth up to argue, he'd find a way to weasel in deeper and I'd tell him my truth, I'd tell him my hurt because men like him always wanted everything.

And then he would leave.

And I would have to come face-to-face with the fact that I wasn't just sad.

I was depressed.

And alone.

Chapter Six

JULIAN

I felt like shit.

The whiskey wasn't doing anything, and I knew sleep wouldn't come, but if I had to sit in silence with that woman for five more minutes, I was going to lose my mind.

Damn, but she was hostile.

And I'd barely spoken to her other than trying to get her the hell out of my cabin and into something new.

She looked vaguely familiar, though I still wasn't sure why. Didn't every pretty girl look the same?

They were all fake anyway.

At least that's what I told myself, because if I actually thought about it, I thought about Isobel, and then I started analyzing every little thing I had done wrong, every situation in which I treated her like an object instead of a person. I'd labeled her as fake because even though she tried, I knew she was never happy as she changed herself to measure up to my father's demands, to mine. I saw her smiles becoming less genuine the longer we were together. It felt easier generalizing all women than looking in the mirror and seeing the guilt in my own eyes.

I punched the pillow and flipped over to my side and shivered. It was freezing in the house, I probably should have set a fire in each of the bedrooms, but I wasn't thinking past my annoyance at the girl who refused to speak to me.

Everyone spoke to me.

I was powerful in every way that mattered. Women threw themselves at me on a regular basis, especially after my falling-out with Izzy. Getting a woman—any woman—to like me wasn't usually a chore, the biggest issue was leaving her in the morning while she slept, not that it was my MO to do so. I hadn't slept around since before the coma, and even then, it had been a giant drunken mistake.

I winced at the memory and shook my head.

I thought if I shared my name with her, she'd be more forthcoming. Instead, it seemed to make her even more irritated.

I'd never had that problem before. If anything, women tended to gain interest the minute they realized how much money I had. I wasn't sure what to do with one who almost seemed to hold it against me.

Another shiver wracked my body. With a muttered curse, I threw the blankets over to the side of the bed and went in search of more firewood. We'd gathered enough to start a fire in my room and hers; at least she'd see I wasn't a complete ass.

I slowly made my way into the dark living room, confusion warring with a bit of annoyance that she'd let the fire go out after only an hour, and then a cold breeze picked up. I glanced toward the door.

Not only was it open, but snow was making its way in.

A chill ran down my spine as I quickly put on my shoes and grabbed my jacket. She wouldn't go out by herself, not at night, right? I mean I'd told her as much earlier, but I had been right there. I was trying to scare her away, not get her killed!

I grabbed my cell and turned on my flashlight as I stomped out into the blizzard. We already had well over a foot and it was still coming down hard. What the hell had she been thinking?

And how long had she been out there?

I rounded the corner and froze. She was lying facedown, the previously white snow now stained red.

I opened my mouth to yell.

But I didn't even know her name, did I?

Breathing another curse, I fell to my knees next to her and felt for a pulse. It was there—barely. "Hey, wake up . . ."

She let out a moan.

Thank God.

"Hey." I shook her lightly. "I need you to wake up. I think you hit your head, and I don't know how long you've been out here."

"Is it gone?"

"Is what gone?"

"The elk." She shivered. "Huge."

"You fought an elk?"

"I lost." Her teeth chattered as she tried to sit, she brought her hands to her lips. The fingers were fire engine red, and looked frozen solid.

Shit.

"Can you walk?" I asked, gently cupping her face with my hands. Blood was sticking to her right cheek and was scabbing near her ear.

She seemed confused, like she wasn't sure if she knew how to answer that question, which only made my panic increase.

The blizzard was bad.

It wasn't stopping.

And she needed better medical attention than I was prepared to give her.

"Come on." I stood and pulled her to her feet. She stumbled against me. Biting back yet another curse, I threw her over my shoulder as gently as I could and made the trek back into the house.

I immediately set her on the floor right in front of the fireplace. "Stay awake, alright?"

She moaned but nodded her head.

I ran as fast as humanly possible back outside to grab more firewood and made it back just in time to see her nod off.

"No!" I yelled, knowing I was being rough. "You have to stay awake, you could have a concussion."

Honestly, I didn't know what she could have.

A concussion?

Internal bleeding?

Her teeth chattered as she blinked her eyes open and tried to focus on me.

I built the fire while watching her out of the corner of my eye, every few seconds she'd close her eyes too long, and I'd grunt.

Apparently, my grunt was terrifying enough for her to jerk awake and glare at me.

Good. I was okay with her anger if it kept her awake long enough for me to try to figure out what the hell to do.

"Cold," she whispered. Her lips were starting to turn blue.

I sighed helplessly and shrugged out of my jacket. "You know I was joking earlier when I said we'd need to use body heat."

She blinked slowly as I pulled my sweater over my body and tossed it on the floor then jerked my sweats down until I was standing in front of her completely naked.

I didn't give her time to process what I was about to do, instead I grabbed one of the down blankets off the couch and spread it behind her, then very gingerly tried to peel off her jacket.

Thankfully, she didn't protest until I made it down to her bra and underwear, which were soaked through.

"I need to take these." I was asking permission from someone who could die if I didn't get her core temperature back to where it needed to be.

She swatted my hand away and then hung her head. "So tired . . ."

"Nope." I patted her left cheek lightly. "Stay awake, princess."

"Princess," she repeated like it disgusted her.

Her snarl was almost endearing as I unhooked her bra and then pulled her against my chest, easing her wet underwear down her legs and mentally apologizing to whomever she belonged to for not just seeing her naked but undressing her, exposing her, and worst of all, looking.

I pulled her freezing body against mine and wrapped the blanket tight around us as we sat in front of the fire. Chills wracked her body as I rubbed up and down her arms.

I needed a plan.

Get her warm, examine her wound, make sure she had all ten fingers and toes then call for help.

Her head lolled to the side like she was going to fall asleep again.

"Nope, sorry, I know you're tired, princess, but we need to get warm, and then I'm going to make sure that you didn't hit your head hard enough to die on me, alright?"

"Didn't." She turned in my arms and clung to my chest, tightly pressing her head against my skin. "So cold. Don't care."

"I know." I rubbed her back. "We'll get you warm, alright?"

"Sleepy."

"No." It was going to be a long night, wasn't it? "I need you to tell me what happened, alright?"

She nodded and then whispered, "He died."

"What?" I froze and pulled away my eyes, searching hers. "Who died?"

"Noah." Her eyes filled with tears. "He died, and I'm alive."

"Had you been in the snow longer . . . ," I said under my breath. "Was Noah your brother?"

Husband? Fiancé? Friend?

She just shook her head. "The elk came, and then I screamed and kicked the wall of the cabin."

I nodded. "Did he hit you?"

"Noah?"

"The elk," I clarified, cupping her cheeks. "I need you to focus. Did the elk hit you in the head?"

"Me?" She shuddered against me. "No, the ice did, from the roof. I think it was ice, something hit my head. The elk ran." She yawned. "Can I sleep now?"

I held her close, my hands on either side of her face as I stared at her pupils. She looked fine, she wasn't puking, but she'd clearly been knocked out. I wasn't sure if I needed to keep her up all night, or just keep waking her up.

With a grimace, I nodded my head. "I'm going to have to keep waking you up every few hours, though, okay?"

"Good thing you're warm," she whispered before nodding off against my chest.

My right arm strained across the floor for my phone.

I set three alarms, each waking me up every two hours.

And then I wrapped my arms around her and prayed the blizzard would end soon, because I was in over my head, and the last thing I needed was another death so close to one I still hadn't recovered from—it was a selfish thought, projecting my anger and fear onto a woman who was most likely just trying to take care of herself and grab some firewood. But that was what happened when a person didn't deal with grief. It found a way to be heard, even if it was unfair. Even if it was wrong.

"You better not die," I said through clenched teeth as I hugged her close.

Chapter Seven

KEATON

I'd never been so hot in my entire life, and just when I was finally comfortable against the furnace I had obviously fallen asleep next to, hands would brace my shoulders annoyingly and wake me up.

At first, I thought it was a bad dream.

I was too tired to care.

I went from freezing to heatstroke all within the span of what felt like an hour, but I couldn't open my eyes, didn't want to, I just wanted to sleep a little bit longer.

"Princess, I know you can hear me, open your eyes and give me a little grunt so I know you're not dead."

Whose voice was that?

Why did it sound so . . . gruff?

Tired and sexy?

I searched my memory, but all I had was the cabin, lying on the couch, grabbing more firewood, and then nothing. I'd been irritated with the owner.

Julian.

Julian.

Tennyson.

I stiffened and then very slowly opened my eyes.

The first thing I saw was fear.

I was so unaccustomed to seeing it reflected in someone else's face that it took me by surprise. I was usually the one trying to hide my fear every time I saw that Noah had lost more weight or gotten weaker.

Why was Julian staring at me like that?

My head pounded. I tried lifting my hand.

"I wouldn't." His arms tightened around me. Why was he holding me? And where was his shirt? "You hit your head."

"Why are you naked?" My voice was hoarse, thick like I hadn't had water in days.

His dark eyebrows shot up. "You're welcome for saving your life."

"Huh?" I blinked up at him. He was pretty, I had to give him that. Green eyes, hair I wanted to run my fingers through, a strong, muscular chest that refused to let me go. *Where does a guy get pecs like that?*

I'd forgotten what it felt like to be held tight.

To feel protected.

And that made me even more traumatized than the fact that I was completely naked in his arms while he stared at me like I was a lunatic. Noah hadn't been able to hold me tight, he was too sick, and now I was being held, and I hated that it was nice.

"What happened?" I was afraid to move.

He sighed. "I couldn't sleep and found you outside by the wood-pile. You said something about an elk and Noah." His lips turned into a small smile. "Unless you named the elk, I highly doubt they're one and the same."

I talked about Noah?

I cleared my throat. "I didn't name the elk."

"Too bad." He sighed. "You were bleeding, I was afraid you had a concussion so I've been waking you up every few hours. The snow just stopped, but we don't have cell service. The towers must be down."

So much information for someone with a pounding headache, sitting naked in a stranger's lap.

I pressed my fingers to my temples. "Okay."

His eyes roamed across my face and then he gently touched the bandage on my right temple. "Your head should be fine, your hands, however . . ."

My hands?

I looked down and gasped.

Through gaps in the bandages around them, I could tell my hands were huge, swollen, red, and angry, and I could barely feel them. "What happened?"

"I think you have frostbite, but I'm not a doctor. I wrapped them and tried to get you warm, but they're not cooperating like the rest of your body."

Tears filled my line of vision. I needed my hands. People needed hands! Especially if people were supposed to type out a story due to an editor in a mere thirty days!

Panic seized my chest as I stared at my hands, a few tears leaked out onto the bandages. "But . . . my book."

"Your book?"

"How am I going to finish my book?" I burst into real tears then. "It was my final promise to him, I promised him! Why would the universe be against this? Against me like it was against him . . ." I started to shake.

"Hey, hey." Julian held my hands in his. He didn't hold them tight, not that I could feel a whole lot. "I won't let anything happen to your hands, okay?"

"Don't make promises you can't keep," I snapped.

His face lost a bit of its arrogance as he looked away and then met my eyes again. "Money buys good doctors, though people still die, that's the sad reality. Money can't buy more time . . . or a healthy body . . ."

His eyes were glassy. "But this is frostbite, you'd let something like that set you back? O wielder of knives?"

I scowled to keep from smiling. "Now I don't have a weapon."

"You never needed a weapon in the first place." He grinned.

I sucked in a sharp breath and broke eye contact. Refusing to let him see the blush that I felt warming my cheeks or the ridiculous notion I had in my head that with a man like him this close to me, I would always need a weapon and armor.

Because Julian Tennyson up close was lethal.

And Julian Tennyson thinking about me, holding me in his arms, felt too good.

I shivered again.

He wrapped the blanket tighter around us. I tried not to think about the fact that I was sitting in his lap like a child, his arms around me, his body keeping me warm.

The fire roared in front of us. "So much for relaxing."

He let out a heavy sigh. "Tell me about it."

"I'm sorry . . ." I felt stupid. "For going out in the snow."

"Look at me," he whispered. "You were getting firewood, hardly a crime, and mere princesses can't control the elk population, though I'm pretty sure you could have beaten him had you not gotten knocked out."

"I went down fighting." I chewed my lower lip and smiled.

"That's how we'll spin the story." He winked. His laugh was gravelly; I felt it low in my belly. "Promise."

"Hopefully, there won't be a story to tell." But even as I said it, I knew there would be a story because he was Julian Tennyson.

And I was Keaton Westbrook.

The press would pay good money for photos of us in the same room.

Add that to the fact that we were both naked.

Nobody could ever know.

It would ruin everything, including the book deal. People didn't forgive you for being human, and they rarely forgave you for moving on with life even though it was a natural thing to do.

"Who's Noah?" he asked.

I ignored him.

And felt his body shut down a bit right along with his interest. It was better this way, better not to let him in.

I was already naked in his arms.

I was already hating my response to him because it was so unlike the way I used to respond to Noah.

I let my guilt project itself into hate, and I directed it at Julian Tennyson, gladly, because it was better than admitting that it was nice.

Being held.

Rather than offering comfort and empty words.

It was nice, too damn nice.

Chapter Eight

JULIAN

She was beautiful when she wasn't being argumentative. Hell, she was beautiful no matter what.

And my body was having a hard time cooperating with the signals my brain was sending, signals like *Injured, Stranger, Don't take advantage.*

I wasn't that guy anymore.

He didn't wake up from the coma.

And any remnants left of the man who would just take what he wanted and move on had died right along with my mother.

I'd buried my past.

Or I'd attempted to.

She was asleep again. She pressed a hand to my chest and held it there like she was waiting for a heartbeat.

She said his name again.

Noah.

I wondered if this Noah realized how lucky he was. To have a woman cry out to him even in her weakest moments, in her sleep, to need him so desperately that she couldn't stop saying his name.

Jealousy hit me hard and fast because I knew my name would never fall from a woman's lips like that.

I was either a checkbook or a business ally. Women wanted me for my money, my power, and my influence.

Finding someone normal only happened once in a lifetime, and look how that had turned out.

"Mmmmm . . ." She lifted her head and then reached her bandaged hands around my neck. "I missed you . . ."

I froze. Dear God, let her wake up.

She moaned again. "Feels so good, right?"

Fuck.

I clenched my jaw as she moved on my lap and then straddled me. Not how I planned on spending my morning. "Princess, you're dreaming . . ."

"It's such a good dream," she argued in a sultry, sleep-filled voice.

My body was on fire.

Shit.

Her forehead touched mine, I could almost taste her, could feel the warmth of her breath on my face.

One touch.

Nobody would know.

We were snowed in.

I was justifying one graze of her lips.

I was going insane.

I muttered a curse and pulled away just as her mouth came crashing down onto mine.

And then I forgot everything.

Everything.

And kissed her back.

Her lips were searing hot, her body molded against mine like it was made for me, and when her tongue slid into my mouth, I thought I was going to die on the spot.

She tasted so fucking good.

So good.

"Mmm . . ." She pulled back. "Noah . . ."

I jerked away.

Lucky bastard.

She thought I was him.

That wasn't cheating.

It was just unfortunate.

"Hey." I shook her by the shoulders a bit. "You were dreaming again."

Her eyes opened so fast that you'd think I told her we had company, and then she stared at my mouth.

Was it red from her kiss?

Swollen?

"See something you like?" I joked.

She rolled her eyes and shoved at my chest. "Sorry."

"What do you have to be sorry for?"

"Inconvenience. And you don't seem like the sort of guy who likes to be inconvenienced. No, you're a planner and I'm ruining your plans."

"Technically, I ruined yours first," I argued and then reached for my phone. "Looks like we still don't have cell service. Do you feel well enough to get dressed and eat something?"

She nodded, her eyes uncertain even as she said, "I think so."

"Take it easy, alright?" I slowly unraveled us and tried like hell not to look at her breasts as I helped her stand.

She slumped against me, body weak. I steadied her and waited, but she just swayed in my arms again.

"Food," I repeated. "You need food. Let's keep you wrapped up, try that first, and then we can see about a shower, okay?"

"I'm not dirty."

My lips twitched. "I didn't say you were, I just thought it might make you feel more like yourself."

Her face changed as she looked away. "Yeah, I haven't felt like myself in a while, I doubt a shower's going to help."

"You never know," I whispered as shadows danced across her face, twirling around secrets I knew she'd never tell a stranger, least of all one like me.

"Pancakes." She changed the subject. "Let's make pancakes. I have enough ingredients and it should warm us up."

"You stay, I'll make the pancakes." I set her back down in front of the fire, forgetting I was naked as I stood. She watched, and my body found great pleasure in being seen. "Ignore . . ." I choked on my next few words as my body acted violently against my brain, showing her exactly what I thought about her smooth skin. "That."

She jerked her head away. "Consider it ignored."

"Huh, that easy?"

"Searching for compliments?" She smiled but didn't look at me.

"Nah, I've lived a life swimming through a sea of compliments, they kind of fall on deaf ears after a while."

She tilted her head up at me. "I know what you mean."

"Does that mean you're going to let me know what your name is?"

She sighed and then very quietly said, "Keaton Westbrook."

I froze.

Stared.

Stared a bit harder.

And then felt like the biggest ass on the planet.

No, worse than that.

The hair that grows on the ass.

"Keaton Westbrook," I repeated.

"The one and only."

"And Noah," I finished, feeling like an even bigger fool.

"Normal Noah." Her eyes filled with tears. It was what the press had dubbed her boyfriend. People were obsessed with their story until a bigger one hit—mine.

47

I should have recognized her the moment I saw her, and then I should have run like hell in the opposite direction.

Everyone knew about her and Normal Noah.

I knew it, and I had been in a coma.

Their love story was front-page news because of her own social media following along with the fact that her parents were celebrities in their own right.

People dubbed Keaton "America's sweetheart" because of how genuinely nice everyone said she was, always doing the right thing, always positive. No wonder he fell in love with her.

Keaton had met the love of her life.

And he tragically died in her arms at the age of twenty-seven.

News reports said they could hear her screams echo through the entire hospital.

It was still front-page news when I woke up from my coma. The first thing I read about, Keaton Westbrook and the love of a lifetime. Meanwhile my brother was sleeping with my fiancée.

And I remember thinking, *It could be worse.*

I could be dead.

Only to look up at the news channel and realize that while I was able to say that, he wasn't.

He'd been in the same hospital.

The news crews followed me like a madman.

And a young girl with a single red rose passed me in the hall with tears streaking her face, and all I kept thinking was how pissed I was at my own family.

So when I ran into her and the rose fell from her hands, I did nothing.

When the petals scattered across the floor, I kept walking.

When her sobbing reached my ears, I ignored it.

And when I watched the news later that night, the guilt came.

His final gift to her.

A single.

Red.

Rose.

After his death she honored him by going every day and bringing roses to cancer patients. And what did I do?

I'd stepped all over the fucking petals.

Chapter Nine

KEATON

His face was stone as he stared down at me like he was putting the pieces of the puzzle together, like he was seconds away from saying something he couldn't take back, like *I'm sorry*.

I didn't want his sorry.

His pity.

Or an apology.

I'd suffered through enough of those, and they were meaningless words people used in order to fill the awkward void at a funeral, or when they didn't know what else to say.

Chills still wracked my body. He pressed in next to me again.

I went from being searing hot to icy cold within seconds. My brain was still sluggish, but not enough that I didn't realize I was very much naked in a friggin' billionaire's arms, and he wasn't pushing me away.

Yet.

My hands felt heavy as they wrapped around his body to keep close. His eyes searched mine before he bit out a curse. "Death is . . ." He looked away. "So very fucking final, isn't it?"

Not the apology I was expecting.

I nodded, my voice would have come out scratchy and hoarse, filled with emotion a stranger didn't deserve, and if I couldn't even cry in front of my own parents . . .

Or at his funeral . . .

Then it would be ridiculous to cry in this man's arms, this man who didn't seem to care about anything but himself.

"The cabin, my cabin," he clarified. "Why did you rent it for thirty days?"

"Vacation," I said quickly.

"Bullshit."

"Why are you here?" I countered.

His lips turned upward into a tense smile. "Same."

"Bullshit."

Julian Tennyson was too good-looking to be naked against me, and my body was too aware of the fact that he had more muscle than I originally thought. I expected him to be soft hands, soft everywhere from too much whiskey and late nights at the office.

He was the exact opposite of soft.

It was a problem.

A growing problem.

I cleared my throat. "So now what?"

"Now . . ." He sighed and looked around. "We pray that our cells start working, and I get you out of here as soon as possible."

I scowled. "A little injury isn't going to get me out of your hair. Unbelievable!" I started to move away from him when he gently pulled my body down. I had no choice but to follow since I was weaker than I expected.

"Listen." He tilted my chin up gently. "I found you passed out in the snow, you have frostbite on your hands, and this is the first time you've been coherent enough to carry on a normal conversation where you don't call me the wrong name."

"What?"

"Not important," he said quickly. "The point is, you need medical attention I can't give you, and I'm not going to let anything happen to you. I wouldn't be able to live with myself if—" He stopped talking, his throat moving in a swallowing motion as he sighed. "You need a doctor. And lucky me, I had some of the best in the city. I'll take you in, and we'll assess the damage."

"And then what?" I whispered. "You come back here, and I lose the cabin for good?"

"Anyone ever told you you're stubborn as hell?"

"It's part of my charm." I blinked my eyelashes at him, thinking it was sexy when it was probably so slow and awkward that it looked like I was inebriated.

"Uh-huh." He licked his full lips. "Guess I'll have to take your word for it, and do you really want to come back up here alone for thirty whole days?"

"You don't understand." Panic set in. "I couldn't do this at home, couldn't get the words out—" Damn it, I felt weak. "I thought being in the one place . . ." I squeezed my eyes shut. "Never mind, you wouldn't understand."

"Rich-girl problems?" He smirked.

"Really?"

"Sorry," he quipped. "Old habits . . . I'm not the most trusting person on the planet."

"Yeah, well, waking up to a world very much changed probably does that to someone . . ."

He was silent and then he whispered, "It really does."

"I need to come back." I tried again. "I promised him and the publisher that gave me an advance that I'd write our story."

His interest seemed piqued as he tilted his head and pulled my body tighter against his. I couldn't think clearly when he was that close, when I could see the gold flecks in his eyes. "I bet that's hard."

"Why would you say that?" I said defensively.

His eyes softened. "Because the story has to end, and you'll have to type the final words that nobody wants to repeat let alone release into the universe . . . The End. You may as well be typing The End of Us, The End of Love, The End of Everything. I don't envy you that, not one bit."

He spoke like he knew of loss. Was he talking about his fiancée? No, there was genuine hurt in his eyes right along with fear and anxiety. It was like looking into a mirror.

I stared at the fur blanket surrounding us. "How about those pancakes?"

"Almost forgot." His smile was forced. "Stay by the fire and I'll be just a minute. Any requests?"

"I'm shocked you can even cook," I teased.

"I can't." He let out a laugh. "So if they taste like shit, eat them anyway and keep my pride intact, yeah?"

I gulped because when he stood to his full height, the fur blanket loosened from my body and pooled around his legs. I sucked in a breath and tried not to look affected, but he was everything I didn't realize I'd been missing in a man.

I wanted to hate him for pointing it out without realizing.

He was healthy.

So healthy.

Strong.

Virile.

With thick legs and corded muscles around his midsection.

Even his color screamed health.

I locked eyes with him and nodded. "I'm starving. Beggars can't be choosers."

"Hmm." He crossed his arms and then gave me a view of his ass as he quickly grabbed a pair of sweats lying across the couch and pulled them on.

I would never admit I was disappointed.

Just like I wouldn't admit that I felt guilty because I stared.

Guilty that I found him attractive.

Guilty that my heart was beating so wildly against my chest.

Guilty that Noah's wasn't.

Guilty that Julian was right.

I didn't want to type the words.

The End.

And a part of me worried . . . I never would.

Chapter Ten

JULIAN

I didn't show any outward reaction, when internally I was a complete mess. What were the odds? Both of us in the same cabin at the same time, miserable, angry, and without electricity until the generator finally kicked on?

She'd lost the love of her life.

And part of me wanted to say, *I know how it feels.*

The staggering conclusion my brain came to had me reeling for the next thirty minutes as I read directions and tried to make pancakes that didn't taste like complete shit.

My mom.

She was the love of my life.

When I thought about loss.

Losing something precious and valuable.

I thought of her.

Only her.

My hands shook as I dumped the batter into the skillet and waited for it to bubble so I could flip it. Keaton had been silent, dozing in and out of sleep. Every few minutes I'd glance over my shoulder to make sure she was alright, and every few minutes I would curse the blanket that kept inching down the right side of her body until I saw nipple.

Not just any nipple.

But the perfect nipple.

I'd seen a lot of naked women in my life, not because I constantly cheated on my fiancée, though I did make one unforgivable mistake, but women had a tendency to pull off their clothes in my presence. Didn't matter if it was a bar, a seedy bathroom, the boardroom—they wanted me to see the goods, and all of them thought the same thing.

If I saw, I'd take.

They had no clue that I didn't give a fuck.

That I'd stopped feeling the minute I realized I couldn't get Isobel back. A drowning man doesn't want more water—he just wants a life raft.

And I'd been drowning so long without any hope of rescue.

Until I almost died.

Should have died.

I snorted and flipped the pancake over and waited while the sun started rising over the horizon. At least three feet of snow covered the mountainside, and what I could see of the outside was so bright that it burned my eyes.

We had at least a day or two before the roads would be clear, maybe more.

I wasn't a doctor by any means, but even I knew that someone needed to check out Keaton's hands before she lost fingers—if it was even that bad, and I prayed it wasn't.

I'd acted fast.

She was alive.

I just had to remind myself of that.

I wouldn't survive another death on my hands.

More blood.

I reached for the pancake without thinking, burning two of my fingers before grabbing the spatula and tossing it onto the plate. I cursed and gave my hand a shake.

"Are you okay?" came a groggy voice from the living room.

She just had to have a sexy voice when all I needed was for her to go back to her annoying self.

"Almost lost a fight with a hot pancake, but other than that, good to go," I said dryly as I crossed the distance between us and held out the plate to her.

Keaton's eyes flashed with excitement as she stood and reached for the plate.

A few things happened at once.

I stumbled in an effort to grab the blanket that was already falling from her body, the pancake wobbled then went flying, and the plate unfortunately crashed to the floor.

My hands caught the blanket at her waist just before it dipped below her hips, and I held it there, like a dumbass, with pancake and glass at my feet.

"Sorry." Her voice was small as she stared at me, and my hands refused to let go of the fur as they very tightly pulled it back around her shoulders and held it there. "My stomach was making all decisions for me."

"You won't hear me complaining," I said honestly. "Though I figure if I look one more time without your permission you're going to go grab that knife and figure out a way to hold it at my throat, frostbite be damned. Am I right?"

Her smile was wide, infectious. "What is it with you and being petrified of knives?"

"Not petrified," I mused. "Just . . . careful when women filled with rage point them at me."

"You were rude."

"So were you."

She huffed.

I stood my ground.

And then she sighed, her shoulders relaxed. "Fine, I'm calling a truce."

"Pancake truce," I added. "We shake over the broken plate and food and start over, how's that sound?"

Her eyes darted from mine to my mouth, then back again. "It's been a while since I've had a fresh start."

"Not for me, I had a coma . . . yay . . ." I said with all the dry humor in the world as I held her gaze.

Keaton bit down on her lip and smiled. "A pancake truce it is."

"What? No insult about my brain injury?"

"Your brain seems to be working just as good as your reflexes." She winked. "And why would I insult the living when it's a direct insult to those who are dead?"

I sobered and looked away. "Good point."

"So . . ." She cleared her throat. "Why don't I get changed, clean up the mess, and we can talk about what this truce entails, you know, since we're stuck here for the unforeseeable future."

I had a vision then.

Maybe it was a flash.

Or just wishful thinking.

I could stay.

With her.

In my family's cabin.

And shut out the rest of the world.

It was insanity.

And yet, it was tempting. Shutting the world away, pretending the pain didn't exist, and being normal.

For once in my life.

Hell, I gathered firewood yesterday, and today I was making pancakes. If Bridge knew what I was doing he would have called the paramedics or worse, asked if I was on drugs.

I smiled. And then I hesitated, not wanting this moment to be broken, whatever the truce meant, we seemed to do better when both of us dropped our guards. Sadly that's something that people like her and me never did.

Unless we were alone.

Forced vulnerability was like staring down hell and then walking right through the flames.

"Deal," I found myself saying. "Go change, I'll clean up the mess."

She sidestepped me and slowly wobbled down the hall to the master suite, where she'd deposited all her stuff. Last night I was ready to toss her suitcase out the door.

This morning I was ready to hide it.

Yeah, I was finally losing it.

My mind.

I knelt down and grabbed the two pieces of broken plate and the still-hot pancake and threw it all in the trash, then went back to the stove and attempted a second pancake.

Apparently I was concentrating too hard because I didn't hear her come back into the kitchen.

"I think I need help," came a grumble from behind me, causing me to jump a foot and spill batter all over the counter. "Is that your thing? Breaking things? Spilling? I'm not complaining, I mean at least it's a flaw. I've been looking for one, you know, other than your stellar personality, for the last few hours . . ."

"When you try your entire life to be perfect . . ." I sighed and then turned around to offer whatever assistance she needed and was suddenly grateful I wasn't holding another plate. "Why aren't you wearing a shirt?"

Her glare said it all as she held a piece of fabric against her breasts. "I can't get . . . something on, before the shirt."

"You got your pants on."

"They're leggings! Hardly rocket science."

"And a T-shirt is?" I refused to look down, stared straight into her pretty eyes. "Why does it feel like you're testing me?"

"Doubt you'd pass even if I were." Her cheeks pinked a bit before she exhaled, causing her lips to make a funny annoyed sound. "Look, I'm not going to walk around here without a bra on, it's freezing and . . ."

I grinned wide. "And?"

"You're an ass."

"I know." I crossed my arms. "So I'm told on a daily basis."

"Lucky you," she said sarcastically. "Pancake truce, you promised. I just need you to close your eyes really tight and help me get my sports bra over my head and down . . . just . . . down. My hands hurt, and they're all wrapped up and swollen, and I tried at least a dozen times before I came out here, don't make me beg."

My body jerked in response as I lazily drank in her irritation, and the way it was directed at me. Was I actually enjoying her anger?

Maybe it was because she wasn't scared of me.

Maybe it was because she was genuine and insulting, and women typically didn't treat me that way.

Maybe it was because I enjoyed her scowl almost as much as I enjoyed her smile.

Even Isobel used to paste a fake smile on her face around me.

Not Keaton.

No, Keaton just kept her claws out, never sheathed them, and found great joy in threatening me.

"I'll help," I found myself saying. "No begging necessary."

She exhaled like she was relieved. "Thanks, here."

I frowned as she handed me a black polka-dotted sports bra that had seen better days. "What's this?"

"What's it look like?" Her voice wobbled in disbelief. "It's my bra!"

"It has a hole!" I pointed with my finger. "You could buy a billion sports bras and you wear this?"

"It's comfortable."

"So is being naked, but you don't see me walking around with my cock hanging out."

"Awww." She patted me on the shoulder. "Got a bit of a problem, Tennyson?"

"Are you insinuating that I have a limp dick?"

"Hey, I'm just here for moral support. If you need to talk, by all means, talk, just do it while helping me get dressed. Then again, it's good to know I'm not in danger of arousing any excitement out of you . . ."

"Too late for that," I said before thinking.

Her mouth shut tight.

I cursed myself to hell. "Turn around so I'm not tempted."

She did a slow circle and dropped her hands to her side. One had the shirt balled in it, the other was empty.

I stared at the bra in my hands.

And then burst out laughing.

"I swear I'm grabbing that knife if you're still making fun of my old ratty bra!"

"No." When was the last time I actually laughed like that? "It's not the bra . . . well, I mean it is, but it's a sports bra. My brain misfired looking for hooks, and then I realized that I'd never in all my life taken a sports bra off someone or put it back on . . . I, uh, got confused."

"It's not a complicated math problem. Just put it over my head."

"Which side does the hole go on?"

"You're the annoying twin, aren't you?"

I narrowed my eyes at the back of her head. "Actually, I'm the charming one."

She looked over her shoulder. "Hmm, can't see it."

"Don't force a demonstration you'll enjoy too much." I winked.

Her lips parted on a gasp as she turned back around and stiffened. "So, let's talk about your ED. When was the first time—"

I jerked her against me, my lips near her ear, barely a whisper away from the skin on her neck. "You don't get to talk about my dick like it doesn't exist. It would be like talking about this." I placed my right hand on her hip and moved it up her skin, my fingers dancing along her ribs until they rested right below her breasts. "And not telling you how very beautiful I find it, not just your skin, but the way it flushes when you get angry or aroused, not that I would know, since you've already rendered me sexless . . ." Her skin broke out in goose bumps. "Now, stand still so I can help you."

She nodded, swaying back against me.

And I wished things were different.

That she wasn't mourning a man I would never compare to or even try to compete with.

That I wasn't mourning a mother I didn't get enough time with, or a life that I no longer recognized.

I wished it was just us.

In that cabin.

Perfect strangers.

Acting on something that felt a hell of a lot better than grief ever did.

Slowly, I lifted the bra over her head and helped her roll it down her body until it was tight against her skin, and then I grabbed the T-shirt from her hands and did the same thing.

Neither of us moved.

Neither of us spoke.

The air felt thick with something that neither of us acknowledged out loud.

I could hear her soft exhale as she slowly turned and faced me. "I won't make fun of you again, but you can't . . ." Her face was pale. "You can't touch me, promise me you won't touch me and we'll be civil . . ."

I narrowed my eyes. "Wrong word."

"Pardon?"

I tucked her hair behind her ear. "You said *touch*, what you meant was *promise you won't tempt me*. Don't worry, princess, those days ended the minute I woke up from that coma."

"What do you mean?" Her eyes rested on my mouth then blinked back up at me.

I grinned. "I'm taking a break from women, which of course means you have my scout's honor I won't seduce you."

She sighed. "Yeah. Good. Great. We should eat." She hurried into the kitchen and grabbed a plate.

"Though . . . offer's on the table, I've never had anyone try seducing me, so fair warning, I wouldn't say no."

The plate shook in her hands as she set it down. "That's not funny."

"I'm not laughing." I pulled out a chair. "Now, let's talk about your hands and the book that you clearly can't write."

When she turned, tears glistened in her eyes. "I'm screwed."

"Lucky for you"—yup, insane, I'd gone insane—"I type fast."

"What?"

"I'll write it."

And in that moment I knew I would write this stranger's ending, and I would help her find closure.

Even though I knew I never would.

Maybe it was my penance.

Maybe it was my mom sending me one last way to make up for my mistakes.

But I knew, clear as day. My job was to help her.

And maybe, just maybe, by doing that, I would earn a bit of myself back. If I stopped her hurt—maybe I'd stop bleeding.

Chapter Eleven

KEATON

"You don't know me," I said dumbly. "Why would you help?"

"Penance for my sins." He didn't smile, just stared at me like his idea wasn't completely crazy. Not only would it mean I would have to actually relive the story and tell it to him, but he'd be writing down my every personal failure and triumph over the last year and a half.

Things I hadn't even told my parents. My mom was my best friend and I hadn't even confessed all of the details to her. I didn't have any close friends because too many people had tried to become my friend because of who I was, and I knew they would turn on me the minute I was no longer useful. I didn't let people get close to me for a reason; I was afraid to trust them with things that mattered.

And there were things, so many things.

Things I hadn't even admitted to myself.

And he would be typing them.

With his hands.

I sat at the table without my pancake as tears filled my eyes. "I could always get some voice software once I'm back in the city." I was bluffing, the last thing I wanted to do was say everything out loud. I had been told that writing would be cathartic.

Saying it felt more real than writing it.

And I was already struggling with writing.

"No, you won't," he said smoothly, leaning his muscled forearms against the table as his dark hair glistened. How did he get it to look so healthy? Thick? And why was I focusing on his hair at a time like this! "Besides, if you haven't noticed, we're stuck here until help comes or until I'm able to call someone, my cell still isn't working, and let's not forget the angry elk that tried to take your life last night."

I felt sick to my stomach as I tried to suck in more air. "You're right, I just . . . I don't know if I can do it. Writing it was hard enough."

He frowned. "Well, how much do you have?"

I laughed because it was so ridiculous. "Oh, you know . . . the title."

"Progress." He winked, was he teasing me? His smile was bright and perfect as he stared at me across the table. "Care to share what it is?"

"It's a working title," I clarified.

"Now we aren't even sure we have a title?"

"Me, not we, there is no we."

"There is now." There was that damn sexy smile again. Had he been born with it or was it practiced in front of a mirror seventy times before he went into board meetings? "Why are you staring at me like that?"

I leaned back in my chair. "Like what?"

"Like you're trying to figure me out." He tilted his head. "Won't work, trust me. What's the title?"

I sighed. Arguing with him was like being stuck in a maze—no matter how many times I thought I found an exit out of the conversation he trapped me again, damn it. He must be hell to live with or negotiate with. "*Losing Him*."

I said it quietly, then I waited for his reaction.

He lowered his head, smile vanishing. "I wonder . . . what it would be like to be missed that much."

"People would miss you, Julian."

"The thing about being in a coma," he said, completely ignoring me, "is that you're not dead, but you're not moving in any direction either. The world doesn't stop just because your body does. And when you wake up, you realize that the world is the same place without you in it, better in some ways you couldn't have expected or accounted for. Most people wake up thankful they're still living, they don't wake up and wonder if it would matter if they were dead."

I couldn't speak.

So I reached across the table with my bandaged right hand. "Only someone who hasn't been told what great value they have would say that. Either you're incredibly stupid, incredibly selfish—"

"Both," he interjected. "At times I think I'm just a little bit both, not for lack of trying to step outside my own world."

"You're not stupid," I said lamely.

He just looked up at me, eyes empty. "I had a woman who loved me, who would do anything for me, and it still wasn't enough. Yes. I'm stupid, very stupid. It would be a disservice to this new friendship of ours to say otherwise."

"Friendship?"

"Well, we are writing a book now . . . though I'll of course give you all the credit, just say something like 'to my pancake-making friend, you know who you are,' in your acknowledgments."

I laughed, thankful for the change of subject. They were dark, the thoughts his mind had, and I didn't know him well enough to make him feel better about the world he lived in, or his place in it.

And the last thing I wanted to do was lie.

"I don't have a choice, do I?" I could practically feel my heart sinking into my stomach at the thought of telling him personal things, things that he would know and write down. And then I felt like an idiot for letting it affect me like that, because soon the world would know it all anyway, so what's the harm in one person knowing before everyone else? Especially if it meant I could get it done faster?

"Not really, no. Plus, I'm not used to being bored, and I'm not one of those people that can just meditate in front of the fireplace and think deep thoughts without wanting to run my head through a wall, so this will be a nice distraction . . ."

"Ah yes, because depressing stories without happy endings are always the way to go when you're snowed in and possibly suffering from frostbite." I snorted.

"Just because you type the end to one story doesn't mean you don't get to start another," he said wisely as he stood and made his way back to the stove. "How much syrup do you want?"

Stunned, I stared at his muscled back. How did someone so wise at times put such a lack of value on his own life? Like he was easily replaceable, when the man I was getting to know was unlike any man I'd ever known.

"Keaton?"

"Sorry," I sputtered. "Lots of syrup."

"She likes sweet things," he commented.

And stupidly the first thoughts that entered my mind were about his smile . . . and then his lips.

Great. Just. Great.

Chapter Twelve

JULIAN

We ate in silence. Her demeanor had changed enough for me to take notice, when I really wished I wouldn't take notice—of anything.

I hated that I normally made a decision about a person within the first few seconds of meeting them. And Keaton? I'd thrown her into the spoiled brat and wannabe Instagram-famous category before she even opened her mouth.

And then quickly transferred her into possibly murderous when she pointed the knife at me.

Now? Now I was noticing something that made me want to look the other way, as if she needed privacy and I was intruding. Privacy to feel, privacy to mourn, to think, to believe the simple lie that there was something she could have done to prevent the death.

The deafening silence of the cabin, of the snow outside, along with the cold, hard reality that we weren't going anywhere anytime soon, had me doing something out of character like reflecting and letting the universe do its thing. God knows I'd spent my entire life trying to manage everything.

And now I was stuck.

Stranded.

And feeling too many things, and watching every single emotion cross her face like I was looking in a mirror, watching my own emotions, experiencing them on repeat while she talked.

"These weren't bad." Keaton offered me a smile as she stood and tried to lift her plate only to stare at it like its shape was offensive.

"I've got dishes." I quickly grabbed her plate and mine and went to deposit them in the sink. "You go get your laptop."

"But—"

"Any better ideas? I mean we could play cards or get naked again if that's your preference?" It was a joke. Kind of. Not really. And even if it was, not very funny, and done in poor taste. It was the insanity rearing its ugly head again.

At least the idea of us being naked was distasteful enough for her to stomp over to the couch, manage to grab her laptop lightly between her bandaged hands, and sit.

I wasn't sure if I was disappointed or offended; then again, one of us needed to keep a clear head, and since mine was still recovering from a month-long coma right along with a broken heart, she wasn't a bad choice in being the rational one.

I turned off the water to the sink, wiped my hands, and made my way toward the couch. She was sitting cross-legged, her simple black T-shirt clinging to her body like a second skin, and her laptop pressing against her chest like she was trying to hug it for comfort. "It's going to hurt."

I sighed and took a seat next to her. "Your hands?"

She shook her head. "My heart."

"Knowledge of pain is knowledge of life . . . it's like cutting off your blood circulation, suddenly you feel nothing, you just watch the blood—life itself—leave a part of your body. The pain you feel later, the tiny prick of needles attacking your skin, is the side effect of healing, it must happen for healing to take place. The pain gives life, and one day, the pain . . . it will stop. Today . . . isn't that day, princess."

She looked at me then, her crystal-blue eyes filled to the rim with tears she looked hell-bent on not shedding. "That was . . ." Her voice cracked. "One of the most logical and beautiful things anyone has said to me since the funeral."

I scowled. "Funerals." The very thought of public mourning of the dead made my skin crawl. Never again.

"Funerals," she agreed in an expressionless tone, but she seemed to flinch at the word. "*Sorry for your loss, Keaton!* Like I lost my phone, or my keys, or my mind. The word gains and loses its power based on the phrases on both sides of loss. *I'm sorry for your loss* says it all, and yet when you hear that, you still hold on to hope that you can find it again. It's a death, not just a personal loss, it's never coming back. Never."

My chest felt heavy as I listened. I didn't want to hear her words. I didn't want to talk about funerals. I was there to forget.

But the universe had other ideas.

Apparently, I was cursed to remember.

And it hurt like fuck.

What would Mom want in this situation?

What would she even do?

Hug her?

Offer more words?

I eyed the computer.

I thought of Mom's easy smile, of her ridiculous obsession with historical romance, and the way she had always seemed to have the shiniest hair despite the lack of vitamins in her system, and I remembered the times I'd find her on this very couch, reading her books, smiling to herself, most likely wishing for her own happily-ever-after.

Dreaming.

Her love for words rivaled her love for life.

And now that she was gone. All I had were words and memories to survive on.

Words.

I didn't question it. I reached out and grabbed Keaton's computer while she watched. I opened it, clicked on Microsoft Word, and started a new document. I typed in "Losing Him," saved it.

And then I wrote.

The power of the word depends on the presence of other words in the sentence, but nothing will ever be as powerful as a word. Nothing lasts forever and reveals more of itself over time as you mature—the written word does. These are Keaton Westbrook's words. Some will hold power, some will take it away, but every single one will bleed with love. Because just like words—love lasts forever.

"What are you typing?" Keaton finally asked.

I turned the laptop toward her and whispered, "The beginning."

Her tears didn't fall, but she covered her mouth with her hands and nodded. "It's perfect."

"You're the one that said it."

"Not that eloquently."

"Where do you want to go next, Keaton Westbrook?"

Her eyes flashed to mine, and then a small smile spread across her lips. "It's going to hurt."

"It's going to hurt." I nodded.

"We go to the beginning . . ." She reached for me with her covered hand. "I just may need more support from a perfect stranger to get through it."

"Please, strangers don't sleep naked together."

"You really need to stop bringing that up when I'm finally warming to you."

I grinned. "You set me up on purpose. The things I could follow that up with . . ."

"Restrain yourself, Romeo." She laughed, a delicate yet somehow full-throated laugh that made me feel . . . way too much. "Okay, okay, we're doing this. This is crazy, but we're doing this. I guess type out 'chapter one'?"

This was insane.

It was also the only time I could ever remember genuinely smiling while looking at a computer.

So I forced my fingers to type it out. *Chapter One: The Beginning of Us.*

Chapter Thirteen

KEATON

I was really doing this, wasn't I? Telling a complete stranger, one I wasn't even sure I liked all that much, something this private? Something this . . . what? Beautiful? Ugly? Real?

He stopped typing and looked up at me. "Ready when you are."

"Why are you doing this?" I leaned in. "You aren't getting anything out of it." He locked eyes with me, and I wasn't sure if he was angry or just thinking of a good reason that wasn't self-serving.

"It's a good distraction." Julian looked away. "Maybe I need one just as much as you do."

"A distraction?" My eyebrows shot up. "Can't you just buy one?"

His lips broke out into a smile that almost made me choke on my own tongue. "Not this kind."

"You mean the sad kind?"

His lips twitched as he seemed to study me, his green eyes so piercing and intense that I felt like I needed to hide behind something. "You're procrastinating."

"No, I'm not," I lied to his face, and then cleared my throat awkwardly because I was doing exactly that.

"Oh." He grinned. "You really are. Look at it this way: you have to get it out somehow. May as well do it when you have someone who's going to pour you a shot every time you finish a chapter."

I snorted. "So you want me drunk?"

"No, I just want you relaxed." He drummed his fingertips against the table and sighed, running a hand through his chocolate hair. "I meant it, about the distraction."

I waited a few beats while he shifted in his seat like he was sitting on a secret and was afraid to spill it.

"My mom." His words were quieter than usual, his posture stiff. "She just died."

I didn't say "sorry," mainly because I knew that sorry wouldn't bring her back, sorry was too easy to say, just like "I love you." Words so casually and callously thrown around lost their meaning fast, especially when you received them from people who would drive a knife into your back when you weren't looking. At least that was my experience in life, words were too damn easy.

"I didn't know," I finally said. "Is that why you came up here?"

He stared down at the table. "It's a lot of the same furniture."

"Here in the cabin?"

He nodded. "Yeah, walking in here was like stepping into the past. I'm not sure what I expected to find."

"Peace." I couldn't stop myself from saying it. His shocked expression met mine briefly before he rested his hands on the keyboard again.

"Well, I'm here." He jutted his chin at me. "I'm trying to find my peace. Maybe it's time you found yours?"

My throat all but closed up as I stared at him, tears in my eyes, tears I fought like hell to keep in. "He stole my breakfast burrito."

Julian let out a low chuckle. "Is that the first sentence or . . ."

I laughed through my tears. "Why don't I tell you the story and we can decide how to write it down?"

"Deal." He crossed his arms.

And I smiled a real smile, one of the first ones in a long time as I told him how I met Noah and how I fell in love.

And Julian listened like it mattered.

Like he cared.

Not the person I would have expected to be sitting across from me the minute I broke my silence on my grief.

A rich playboy.

Who refused to let me say no.

Chapter Fourteen

JULIAN

There's something extremely humbling about hearing someone list the attributes and talents of a person who seemingly had no faults.

That was Noah to Keaton.

The perfect man, best friend, confidant, all wrapped up into one shiny package.

The guy had teased her relentlessly when they first met, stole her food when she was volunteering at the hospital, and then called her out for taking a selfie in the hallway. He told her that it wasn't appropriate with the patients walking in the background.

He'd been wearing Hawaiian board shorts and a shirt that said *Wicked Cool*.

He always wore flip-flops.

And he always smiled.

He was exactly the opposite of who I imagined a girl like Keaton would date. I mean Hawaiian clothes and flip-flops versus a celeb on his private jet? I envisioned her with a celebrity or a male model, maybe even an athlete, not a Hawaiian-shorts-wearing self-proclaimed *Star Wars* nerd who had a burrito obsession and wasn't afraid to call her out.

I finished writing her first chapter. It wasn't perfect, I wasn't an author, but it was good enough for her to weed through when the time came. We'd finished over an hour ago, and all I kept thinking was that Noah had been a lucky bastard and where the hell do I get some Hawaiian shorts so she laughs with me like that?

Her laughter was musical, and when she talked about him, her eyes lit up like shiny blue crystals. That man had earned every single laugh just like she earned every single tear she refused to shed. She held him up on this perfect pedestal, and I wondered what it would feel like to be talked about that way. The way she described Noah, the way I talked about my mom. What would people say about me? The thought was uncomfortable, to say the least. My father had done an excellent job of smearing my name all over even though most people knew it was his jealousy speaking. Bridge and I were doing better financially than he ever did, and he knew it.

I needed to be alone with my thoughts, so I made an excuse about going outside to check for better cell reception.

The snow still hadn't melted, but at least the sun was out, and I wondered how long we would have to wait before we could leave and if it made me a selfish bastard to wish for just one more day, maybe two, where it was just us, no outside world.

The business side of my brain was panicking that I wasn't stressing over a quiet cell phone, but my soul for the first time in years felt settled. I had no idea if the feeling would follow me back into the city, but I highly doubted it.

There was a reason we had a cabin, after all.

Silence.

Privacy.

I looked down at my cell and waited for a bar to pop up. My signal wasn't strong, but at least I had something. My fingers hesitated over the screen.

What the hell was I thinking?

A day ago, I was ready to pay her to leave, and now I was hesitating on calling for help? On finding another place to stay to gather all the fucked-up things in my head?

Her head was fine, and her hands seemed to be healing, right?

I cursed and slid my phone back into my pocket then jerked the cabin door open and stomped the snow off my boots. "No signal." The lie fell easily from my lips.

Keaton frowned at her own phone. "Me neither. Did it help going outside?"

"No." Damn, lying always came way too easy for me, didn't it? Maybe that was the problem. In all of my efforts to please my dad, I'd also inherited some of his worst qualities, manipulation and lying being two of them.

I was nothing like Noah.

I would have destroyed him with one hard Wall Street glance and looked down at him for not owning a suit.

Which just proved how wrong a man like me would be for Keaton, not that I was tempted.

At all.

She smiled up at me and grabbed the bottle of whiskey between her two wrapped hands. "You did promise me a shot if we finished a chapter."

I found myself smiling at her giddiness, which I sensed wasn't just because of the promise of alcohol, but the fact that she'd started their story.

"Why don't I check on your hands first?" I offered.

"Ah, so he's an author *and* a doctor now?" she said, looking even more ridiculous with her wrapped hands on her hips than she probably realized.

"He is." I sighed and walked over to the leather couch. "Sit and I'll unwrap the gauze and see how bad the damage is. Does it hurt?"

Keaton chewed her bottom lip and held out her hands. "Not really. Is that a bad sign or a good sign?"

"If I had Google I'd be able to tell you that." I gently grasped her right hand. "But since I don't, and because I never got my medical license but did something stupid like graduate with honors in business, I'm just going to have to guess."

"What every patient wants to hear. Truly," Keaton muttered under her breath, and an answering smile crept over my face again.

I quickly sobered when I got my first glimpse of the skin on her hands. Everything was still angry red, and she had small sores on her pinky as well as her thumb and forefinger.

"I can't look." She squeezed her eyes shut while I rewrapped her right hand. "Are both hands bad?"

I winced when I unwrapped her left hand. It had somehow taken the brunt of the damage. Every finger had an angry red sore on it, and they seemed swollen too.

"Is your silence good or bad?" Her eyes were still shut.

"It's . . ." I quickly wrapped up her left hand. "It's going to take a while to heal, that's all."

"How am I supposed to do any normal human activity if I can't even pick up stuff off the floor or take a shower or—" Her eyes went wide. "I can't just go thirty days without washing my hair!"

"Careful, your rich girl is showing," I said in a singsong voice, earning a glare from her. "And we aren't stuck here thirty days. A few days at most."

"Since I'm injured, that means I go back into the city and give you what you finally want."

I narrowed my eyes. "What's that?"

"The cabin all to yourself." She sounded defeated.

"I'm not the one who fought with an elk and lived to tell about it. Think about all your Instagram stories!" I crossed my arms and searched her eyes. "Social media gold, right?"

She wasn't laughing.

"Look . . ." My fingertips slid across the leather couch and pressed into her thigh. "Let's just get through today, tomorrow will have its own worries."

She stared down at my hand and whispered, "He used to say that."

Of course the bastard did. "So you're saying he was wise like me?"

"Yeah, but you have him beat in arrogance."

"At least I'm winning at something."

"Is that winning, though?" She snorted out a laugh, and then pointed at the booze. "I want my prize now."

"Do you want me to just pour it into your gaping mouth since you can't hold a shot glass very well?" I teased.

"No, because with my luck you'd just keep pouring." Her eyes narrowed.

"What would be my purpose in getting you drunk?" I unscrewed the cap. "Besides, you seem to be one of those people who'd be chatty when drunk, who don't shut up and decide everyone needs a hug, then after one more shot of tequila and two more rounds of karaoke decide they're going to join the Peace Corps." I sighed.

"Wow." Her lips spread into a thin smile. "That was both insulting and alarmingly detailed."

I lifted the bottle into the air. "I doubt I'm wrong."

She opened her mouth and tilted her head back. I studied her chin of all things. It was smooth just like the rest of her. Her snowy white skin was flawless, her lips plump enough to probably give life during a kiss, and yet her chin is what distracted me, maybe it was the angle or just the fact that she was teasing me. I liked it.

I liked her.

And I realized I hadn't had this feeling in a really long time.

I, Julian Tennyson, had a fucking crush.

I took a long drag of the whiskey, wiped my mouth, then quickly poured some into her mouth.

She choked a solid minute before glaring at me with watery eyes and then kicking me in the shin.

"What the hell!" I roared. "I gave you your shot!"

"You didn't even warn me! I couldn't see you. I was tilting my head back then suddenly fire-burning whiskey from hell cascades down my throat like a lava waterfall!"

I made a face. "Okay, first off, it was maybe half a shot, second, you looked prepared, third . . ." I sighed and ran a hand through my hair. "If you must know, I was distracted."

"By what?"

"Your mouth was open, I was imagining—"

"I will feed you to the elk outside if you finish that with what I think you were going to say!"

I smirked and leaned in. "Dirty mind, rich girl. I was going to say I was imagining touching the skin just below your lips."

She squinted at me. "So you're saying you have a chin fetish."

"A fetish would mean I have a thing with everyone's chins, and I can honestly say I've never given them much notice, but I noticed yours, and your skin, and the way you look like you want to strangle me regardless of how much I'm already helping you."

She rolled her eyes. "It's because I know guys like you, guys who rule the world one hospital donation at a time."

I shifted uncomfortably in my seat because, yes, I did do that. I donated so I didn't feel guilty for not doing more.

"Let me guess, shark in the boardroom, shakes hands at events, takes nice pictures, loves a good tailored suit, and sends food back when it's cooked wrong."

I opened my mouth. Closed it. Then glared. "Okay, first off, if you're paying for a good meal—"

"I knew it!" She thrust one of her bandaged hands in my face. "I know your type, I used to date your type. If you tell me you order the most expensive wine on the menu we can no longer have a working relationship." She crossed her arms while I lazily eyed her up and down then tilted my head back and took another swig.

"Whiskey over expensive wine any day."

She reached out and pressed her right heavily gauzed hand to my chin and swiped. "I figured you weren't saving that."

"What?"

"Two wasteful drops of whiskey, on your chin." She pointed with her paw while I scowled and looked away.

Maybe it was the two shots, maybe it was something else, maybe it was even the magic of Mom still existing within the walls of that cabin, but I found myself hating the way Keaton saw me and my life.

What was worse, I hated that she was half right.

I was that guy.

I had always been that guy.

And that guy got completely screwed, so who was I now? That was the question, wasn't it? I no longer had this need for my father's approval, I owned part of the company, and now I had no fiancée, no pet—not that I'd even had one to begin with—had just moved into a new apartment, and everything felt . . .

Empty.

"I have a thought," I said before I could stop myself.

"Is that what you call it when a light bulb appears over your head?" she teased.

I ignored her and pressed on. "We owe it to each other to stop making snap judgments and just . . . get to know one another."

"Sounds like a date to me."

"If dating means we're napping this afternoon, playing a wild game of chess, and then eating dinner together, sure, but typically I like to be more adventurous on my dates."

"Adventurous like getting chased by an elk?"

"Still stuck on that?"

She held up her hands.

"Right." I smiled at her. "Too soon?"

"You think?"

My smile just widened. "We're stuck here and we may as well find a way to get along. No blood was shed during chapter one, do you think we can manage to sheathe the claws when we're not writing too?"

"That depends . . ." She leaned in.

I sucked in a sharp breath and waited like an idiot.

"What are you cooking for dinner?"

"What makes you think I'm cooking?"

She showed me her hands again.

"You can use your mouth still," I pointed out.

"And you can shut yours," she fired back. "I like pasta."

"Me too."

Neither of us moved.

I sighed. "Fine, I'll play you for it."

"What are we playing?"

I shot her an evil grin. "Strip poker. Whoever keeps the majority of their clothes on wins."

"I know how it works." She rolled her eyes. "I also know that the game could go on forever."

"Five hands."

"Just five?"

"Just five." I eyed her up and down. "And right now it looks like at the very worst you'll be out an ugly sweater, furry socks, and leggings that have holes in them."

That earned me a glare straight from the pits of hell.

"First off, I like my sweater, second, the socks keep me warm, and third, we all have our favorite sweats!"

"Not all of us." I grinned. "Tell me, are you the sort of girl who wears workout clothes but doesn't even have a gym membership?"

Her cheeks reddened.

"Hmm . . ." I winked. "Do you always blush when you're uncomfortable?"

"Guhhhhhhh." She threw her hands up. "Fine, we play five hands. Also it should be noted, I'm a savant with numbers."

"I'm a Mensa member, but cool story."

"You can't see because of the gauze, but I'm holding up both middle fingers and praying you get syphilis."

"And you can't see inside my head, but I'm already celebrating my victory, hope you know how to cook with paws."

She stuck out her tongue and stood. "Where are the cards?"

I almost said, *"Where they always are,"* but I realized quickly this wasn't a thing, me and her vacationing here, or even hanging out here. She wasn't family, she wasn't anything.

Just a perfect stranger.

A really pretty one.

"In the top drawer of the coffee table. You'll find a few stacks, choose wisely, you never know if I've marked the deck."

"If you were a Mensa member you wouldn't have to," she argued.

I burst out laughing. "Get ready to strip."

"Bet that works on none of the girls." She grabbed the cards and made her way back to the kitchen table.

"It works on enough of them." I gave her a smug grin.

"Gross."

I leaned close and captured her gaze. "Keaton, I can guarantee you that *gross* is not a word ever exchanged between me and any female. More like *Wow, oh God*—"

The paw was back, this time covering my mouth. "Stop talking and deal."

I grinned against the medicinal gauze and nodded my head. She pulled her hand back, and her eyes darted away.

And I had to wonder if I made her uncomfortable, or if she was suddenly skittish because she'd touched me and—even with an injured hand—liked it a little too much.

Chapter Fifteen

KEATON

The heart wants what it wants. I knew that better than anyone, but my heart wasn't the issue. It was my eyes and my treacherous body and the way it felt a hit of adrenaline each time Julian touched me.

Even the gentlest touch set me off.

I hated my body for responding to anything he did; it felt like a direct betrayal of Noah even though I knew logically I would eventually have to move on. Eventually I'd live the life we'd planned but with another man.

The thought brought me back to reality and away from Julian's soft touches and teasing remarks.

I was at that cabin for a reason, and that reason was not to crush on a playboy who probably had enough notches in his bedpost to break the frame.

Besides, we were on round five.

He won the first three.

I won the fourth.

"You're staring awful hard at your cards . . ."

"It's not my fault I keep getting distracted by your polka-dotted bra. Didn't notice the little bow on it before. I like it. Did your mom buy you a lollipop before or after she took you shopping at Target?"

I scowled and looked down at my cards. "First off, you're the one who said that socks are a pair and count as one. Second, if you don't like it, don't look." The last thing I needed was another go around with Julian helping me get the bra back on—I barely survived the first time. "And third, this is Victoria's Secret. Oh, and fourth, you're an ass."

"Victoria's Secret," he repeated, his eyes skimming his cards and then the upper half of my mostly bare body before looking back down again. "Wouldn't have guessed."

I shivered and changed the subject. "So? What will it be?"

"All in." He shoved all his M&M's, aka his chips, to the middle of the table, his grin so smug it was almost cute—almost.

I looked down at my cards again. I had a pair of sevens. That was it. I narrowed my eyes at him. Did he have a tell? Businessmen were typically boardroom warriors with nerves of steel, so I highly doubted he'd reveal anything in a card game.

He scratched the back of his head.

Bingo.

I shoved my candy forward. "Call."

"Show me your cards."

"You first." I grinned.

He shook his head and flipped his cards over. "Royal flush."

I slowly lowered my cards and watched in horror as he took all the candy to his side of the table and then very annoyingly jerked his head at me. "Your pants or your bra, your choice."

I shoved my chair back and stood, then gave him an apologetic smile. "Sorry, but"—I held up my hands—"it's really hard to get undressed with all the gauze."

"Yet you managed to get semi-dressed this morning and take your sweater off . . ."

I shrugged. "They're throbbing like I have ten tiny heartbeats."

"Okay." He stood and faced me. "Then I guess I'll have to help you."

Not the direction I thought he'd take. If anything, I thought he'd toss some irritated words my way and stomp out of the room.

"Umm . . ."

He reached for me.

And idiot that I was.

I didn't stop him.

His hands grazed my hips as he held my swaying body steady.

It had been too long, hadn't it? Since I'd been touched, since I'd liked it.

Way too long.

And now my body was misfiring at the worst possible time with the worst possible person on the planet.

"Wh-what are you doing?" My voice was too breathless, my eyes couldn't decide if they should focus on his eyes or his mouth, with its perfect sensual lips, that was inches away from my face.

He leaned in until our foreheads touched and whispered, "Winning." Right before digging his fingers into my leggings and very slowly rolling them down until he reached my bare feet. He gently lifted each foot and pulled them completely off, leaving me standing there in my polka-dot bra and my hot-pink panties. Clearly I hadn't been planning on being naked when I'd packed for this trip. Otherwise, I would have brought something that didn't look like a preteen training bra.

Then again, what was I thinking?

I wasn't ready for that.

For any of it.

It was too raw, too soon.

And again, he was too wrong.

"I'll give these back on one condition." He dangled the leggings in between our bodies.

"Oh, and what's that?" I croaked and cleared my throat. "Because this is as naked as I get."

"I wonder if that makes bedroom activities difficult."

"A truly talented man would work with it," I countered as his eyebrows shot up his forehead.

"I can't decide if that's a challenge or not . . ."

"Not," I said helpfully.

He chuckled. "Fine, it's going to sound stupid, but I'm going to ask anyway."

"Now you have me worried," I teased.

"Kiss me." He said it so quietly I almost didn't hear him. "Kiss me and I'll make dinner and give you back your pants."

"What?"

"A kiss, usually it's two mouths, one soul—"

"I know what a kiss is. I'm just confused, why would you want to kiss me?"

"Let's just call it an experiment. I haven't really kissed anyone since I woke up feeling like a different man, and I want to see if everything on the outside feels the same as it does on the inside—changed."

I hesitated then asked, "Why a kiss?"

His lips pressed into a smile. "Because it's the only thing that exists in this universe that tells you everything without saying a word."

I swallowed the dryness in my throat. "Yeah, next time lead with that."

"Noted." He tilted my chin with his thumb. "Is that a yes?"

"It's just a kiss," I said, more to myself than him. "One kiss. It means nothing."

"Absolutely nothing," he agreed.

"Fine." I licked my lips and waited.

And of course he took his time.

He didn't lean in and press his lips against mine. That would be too easy, and I was beginning to understand that *easy* wasn't in Julian

Tennyson's vocabulary. He smoothed my cheeks with his hands then ran them down my neck only to slowly pull me against his rock-hard chest while his mouth pressed against my neck like he was breathing me in.

My knees shook while I tried to rein in the shiver that was slowly spreading down my legs to my toes. His lips brushed against mine. The feeling was so foreign, I hadn't kissed anyone since Noah. My dreams didn't count.

This was a full-on assault of all of my senses, and he was barely touching me.

His lower lip slid against mine, and then he was kissing me, kissing me so achingly slow that my chest hurt.

He said a kiss spoke without using words.

And his absolutely screamed *ache*.

It wrecked me, ruined my resolve, and made me weak because I was that girl—the one that wanted to fix all the things. I'd wanted to fix Noah and make him better, and even though Julian's hurt was obviously different, a part of him was still broken.

And I wasn't stupid enough to believe a kiss would fix it, but it would at least soothe the ache, that's what affection did to a person's soul, it took the sting away.

I deepened the kiss without thinking.

Wrapped my arms around his neck.

And didn't even realize I was airborne until my butt hit the countertop as his mouth pressed harder against mine, searching as his lips demanded more.

I said one kiss.

This was multiple.

Then again, his lips never left mine.

Did it count?

Why was I overthinking this rather than enjoying the sensation of the best kiss of my life?

I shoved him away as gently as I could. Guilt descended like a choking fog. Logically I knew I hadn't just cheated.

But it felt wrong.

Because it felt so good.

So right.

"So . . ." I could barely keep the tremor out of my voice as I looked up at him. "What did my kiss say?"

His eyes searched mine, and then he very gently leaned in and kissed my cheek, whispering in my ear, "Sad."

Chapter Sixteen

JULIAN

My first kiss had been in that cabin.

My first real kiss.

I'd brought a friend from school—one I wanted to be my girlfriend. We stayed up late, and one thing led to another, we broke into my parents' liquor cabinet, drank way too much peppermint schnapps, and ended up making out on the couch like the horny teenagers we were.

I chuckled and ate another bite of pasta.

Keaton had been oddly quiet ever since I kissed her. I refused to apologize for something that felt so right.

"What's funny?" She yawned behind her hand. "Good pasta, by the way."

I smiled. "Took you three servings to figure that out?"

She ignored me, I was getting used to it. Old Julian would have been livid if he'd been waved off the way she did it, but for some reason I enjoyed it because I knew it meant she was uncomfortable or irritated, which also meant she wasn't kissing my ass. I'd had enough ass-kissing to last me a lifetime.

Perfect, next I was probably going to ask to braid her hair, then pull said braid in order to prove to her that I liked her. My future was bright!

I cleared my throat. "I was just thinking about the last time I had a girl here."

"Wow."

"Jealous?"

"Extremely. Did you even know her last name?"

"Higgins," I said quickly. "And I was fourteen, so before you start imagining strippers and dollar bills . . ."

"Fourteen?" she said, ignoring the stripper comment. "That was the last time you were here?"

I nodded and poured her another glass of wine since her glass was empty. Plus it gave me something to do with my hands, and I found that anytime the subject floated back toward me and my past, I felt fidgety. "My parents divorced that same year, and it was too painful to come back. Some of my favorite memories were with my family, with my brother and my mom. Dad usually showed up for a day tops, then left with another emergency at the office. It was the only time I could ever—" I stopped myself.

Too late.

She leaned forward. "It was the only time you could ever what?"

I sighed. "Be myself."

"That's tragic."

"Yeah, well, so is high school," I joked. "I put a lot of pressure on myself to prove I could handle the company. I swear I was born with a calculator in one hand and a spreadsheet in the other."

"And did you?"

"Hmm?"

"Prove yourself?" she asked, resting her forearms on the table. The sky was getting dark, and I could see new snow starting to fall. Even though we finally had cell service, it looked like we were in for another night together without rescue.

"Well . . ." I swirled the wine in my glass. "That depends. According to him it will be a cold day in hell before I'm ever on his level—but if you look at what I've done with the company, the stocks, the portfolio, and projections for—"

Keaton closed her eyes and started to snore.

"Oh, I'm sorry. Was I boring you?"

She opened one eye and then the other. "I asked about you proving yourself, and now you're talking about portfolios . . . It's a simple question. Did you accomplish what you set out to do?"

I licked my dry lips. "Unfortunately, yes."

God, where was more alcohol or a sedative when I needed it?

I didn't want to travel down memory lane.

I sure as hell didn't want to talk about myself, my shortcomings, or my fears.

It was easy when she was the focus of conversation.

Damn it.

"Why is that unfortunate?" she asked, holding her wineglass with both hands.

"Because . . ." I was seconds away from claiming a migraine when I eyed the computer. She'd told me her beginning; it wouldn't be fair to lie about my end, would it? "That's it, the case is closed. I had one singular goal in life. I accomplished it, and now I'm at the end of a road, and I can't find it in myself to do anything but stand there."

"Is standing there so bad?"

"Yeah, it is, especially when you've been running during your entire existence. What do you do when you realize that accomplishing everything you set out to do leaves you feeling just as empty as you were before, or even more so?" She was quiet, her eyes searching mine. "My brother says I need a hobby."

"A man without a destination isn't lost . . ." She shrugged. "He's just exploring."

"Well, exploring feels a hell of a lot like being lost."

"Do you like it?"

"Being lost?"

"No."

She set her wine down. "Your job, do you like it?"

It was on the tip of my tongue to blurt out yes then laugh at her for even asking such a stupid question. I was incredible at my job. I was rich. I made other people rich. People knew me.

Not the real me.

Not the me I wanted them to actually know or care about.

I sighed. "There's this park bench I used to pass on my run every morning. An elderly lady used to sit there with a purple jacket, purple hat, a cane, full makeup, and a bag of bread. She was there every day feeding the birds, even in a torrential downpour, and then one day she was just . . . gone."

"What happened?"

"I don't know." My throat felt thick. "But I noticed. And I bet other people noticed too, because she was the sort of person you took notice of. And I couldn't help but wonder, after a few weeks of her absence, why it bothered me so much."

She leaned in. "Why did it? She was a stranger."

My smile was sad as I looked away. "Because it made me wonder if I possessed enough redeeming qualities for anyone to miss me. They'd miss the money, the lavish parties, they'd miss the attention—but would they miss *me*? And then"—I stood and grabbed my plate—"the worst happened, I almost died, and I woke to find out that the world not only couldn't care less about my absence, but it was better without me in it. My brother was better at my job, and it took exactly four weeks for my fiancée of three years to fall in love with him. The world, it seemed, didn't need Julian Tennyson, and I've been struggling with that truth ever since." I put my dishes in the sink and gave a defeated smile. "I, um, I'm going to head to bed."

Keaton quickly stood and made her way over to me. Without speaking, she pulled me into her arms and hugged me, then whispered against my chest, "You're wrong."

Chapter Seventeen

KEATON

"No. I will not go out with you," I said for the thirty-second time as Noah followed me down the hall, a long-stem red rose between his teeth. I stopped at the nurses' station and sighed. "He's behind me, isn't he?"

The rose made its way to about an inch from my face. The insane patient was dangling it like a carrot. This was the third week I had been forced to put up with him.

I gritted my teeth and turned just as he moved to his knees and said, "The cancer hasn't killed me yet, but you just might if you say no . . ."

I hid my smile behind my hand and shook my head. "You're relentless."

"I'm in love."

"Oh, dear God." I burst out laughing. "You don't know me! I've been here twice."

"Three times," he corrected, his sandy-brown hair falling across his forehead. He was adorable even though I refused to admit it out loud. "The first time was when—"

"We don't need to rehash the burrito incident."

"Our hands grazed each other, and you know you did it on purpose."

"Are you fifteen?"

"Twenty-six." He grinned wider, his white, straight teeth almost blinding. "If you don't say yes, I might start singing . . ." Behind me, the nurses groaned. "Hey, I have a wonderful voice!"

"Wear earplugs," a nurse piped up. "Or just say yes and save us all from putting them in."

I shook my head. "One date. That's it."

He stood and held out his hand. "Well, let's go, time's wasting."

"Now?" I panicked and looked around me.

He pulled me down the hall. "Time's wasting, K. This is called living. Why don't we try together?"

Great, he already had a nickname for me. "Living?"

"Spontaneous living, because the clock stops for no one, and I like you. You have a beautiful smile and a big heart. And I know you like me even though you keep rolling your eyes. I'll win you over. I'm told I'm very persuasive."

"Or annoying," I offered.

He squeezed my hand and stopped, then turned to face me. I hadn't realized until that moment how tall he was, or how good-looking, maybe because I didn't want to acknowledge any of it. I was horrible at dating, and he was a patient at the hospital.

"Life is meant to be celebrated, Keats, annoying cancer patient and all." He winked and then twirled me and dipped me in the middle of the hallway. His lips pressed onto my neck like they'd been there a million times. The kiss was light, it was perfect. And it was the first time I felt that feeling you get when you're with your person, the person you were destined to be with.

I was his.

And in that moment, he knew it.

"I have Twinkies and a chessboard." He wiggled his eyebrows. "But don't tell my nurses. Apparently multiple Twinkies are frowned upon."

"Multiple? How many do you eat?"

"In a day?" He seemed amused. "Only ten, maybe twelve if I'm feeling fancy. Come on, let's go, time's wasting. Oh, one more thing." He tapped *my nose. "When you fall in love with me, and I promise you will, try not to be sad when I die."*

Horror washed over me. "What sort of—"

He silenced me with a hug and said, "Promise."

I was already in his web.

I was already that far gone.

It took Noah minutes to win me.

And the universe took him away in a single heartbeat.

That is something I won't ever find it in my soul to forgive.

Julian typed the last part of the paragraph and looked up at me. I knew he'd see the sheen of tears in my eyes, and the sheer strength it took to resist letting them fall.

"It's okay to mourn him."

"I don't think I would stop," I admitted.

"Mourning?"

I shook my head sadly. "Crying."

"Would he want you to cry over him?"

I smiled. "No, he'd be pissed. It was one of his things: don't waste tears on stuff you can't change, stay hydrated." I did a lame fist pump. "He seriously said that entire sentence to me with a straight face."

Julian burst out laughing. "I think I would have liked Noah."

"I'm sure the feeling would have been mutual."

Julian made a face. "Just how much do you know about me? I mean other than the rich-playboy thing you keep tossing in my face. Thanks, by the way."

I was so thankful for the subject change that I relaxed in my chair. It was late afternoon, and we'd already been through two chapters. Things were getting easier, or maybe as easy as they were going to get, all things considered.

I studied him a bit then sighed. "Well, I know you're rich, I know you almost died in a head-on collision, went into a coma, came back not really the same . . ."

He barked out a laugh. "You wouldn't have liked me precoma."

"News flash: I barely like you now," I teased.

It earned me another devastating smile from his side of the table. It was hard not to study him, the way his body moved, muscles rippling in his forearms like he couldn't help it, and that playful grin that could turn serious and intimidating in a heartbeat.

"I would have used you." Julian said it like using people for his own benefit was an everyday thing. "I may have cheated on her with you if I was tempted, and I was tempted often. I would have done everything in my power to make you like me, and I would have probably gotten bored by you or felt guilty for how I treated you, maybe both. You would have made my dad jealous, furious actually. He was always competing with me. I was skewed by a false sense of reality. I was taught as a Tennyson that the world was mine and rules didn't apply. No, Noah would not have liked me—he would have seen right through me."

I gulped, trying to digest the information he set on the table like a heavy bag full of his past sins. It lodged itself between us and just sat there. "What made you change?"

"Waking up from the coma. You know, that and the fact that my mom beat some sense and logic into me, reminding me where I came from, what my purpose was. I went to the hospital every day, and every day she gave me a lecture and a challenge to be better. That was more than a year ago, when we first reconnected."

"And in that entire time, the old you never popped up and said screw it all?" I wondered as I picked at my thumbnail and folded my hands in my lap to keep from fidgeting.

His intense stare was back, the one that made my stomach erupt into butterflies and my guilt double up on itself for even reacting that way.

"Well . . ." His smile was crooked, it made him look playful, sexy. Noah would have said Julian looked ready for a photo shoot and probably got manicures on the regular, and he would have probably been right, but Julian didn't seem to shy away from that ugly side of him. He didn't care. "I did yell at my brother and ex a few times, I may have flipped over a desk in my office and gotten painfully drunk a few days in a row, and thrown a mild temper tantrum at the Four Seasons, where security had to escort me to my room, but other than that, nah . . . not tempted."

I burst out laughing. "You threw a temper tantrum at the Four Seasons? What, did your mini bar run out of peanuts?"

"Funny," he said sarcastically, "and no. If you must know, I was also drunk and pissed off. Apparently seeing your ex marry your twin brother does that to a person, and I wanted more M&M's. Can you believe they refused to deliver them to my room?"

"Monsters."

"I used more colorful language at the time." He shrugged. "And should have probably gotten arrested for assault, but I'm a Tennyson. Rules don't apply to me." He seemed disgusted by that.

"I know what that's like," I said softly, and I did. People were always watching and saying how wonderful I was. The scary part is trying to maintain that level of perfection—the scary part is the failing and risking everyone turning against you. Fame is a ticking time bomb, and I knew it was only a matter of time before I fell—or was pushed—from my social media pedestal. "I'm a Westbrook, goody-two-shoes daughter of Hollywood royalty. I can do no wrong."

"I bet I could dirty up that reputation a bit for you." He seemed almost sad about it. "Trust me, hanging out with me would be enough."

I frowned. Hadn't I thought that same thing earlier? How the press would have a field day if they saw us together in the same room? But now . . . now that I saw him differently, I didn't want to think that, refused to believe it. "I don't really think that's true."

"Clearly you haven't been reading the newspapers . . . My dad's still bitter and finds great joy in uncovering every sin I've ever committed and leaking it to the media. The idea that I have his blood in my body makes me want to slit my own wrists."

"Harsh."

"True!" he fired back. "Anyway, sorry, didn't mean to travel down memory lane like that. They aren't fun ones anyway."

"And mine are?"

"Good point." He laughed. "At least yours are good ones, solid ones you want to hold on to forever."

"That's the thing about memories. They always fade, don't they?"

He was quiet and then said, "That's why you talk about them, that's why you're writing this down. Your words keep his memory alive."

I sucked in a sharp breath. "Yeah."

"Hey, Keaton?"

"Hmm?" I didn't want him to see me get emotional again, but it was impossible not to look at Julian when he spoke to me, almost like I was doing my body a disservice by not making eye contact.

He walked around the table and then pressed a kiss to the top of my head. "Only the luckiest of men die knowing they lived even a few days with a love like this." His smile was so sad my heart pressed against my chest like it needed to escape, needed to reach out to him, be the salve to his still gaping wound.

Both of us were broken.

But in different ways.

He was mourning the loss of not just his mom, but of his past, of the time he misused as the man he'd been.

I was mourning a love that ended too soon, like a flower that never gets to fully bloom.

I wondered if it was all the same, because it was painful no matter the reasoning behind it, and pain couldn't lie dormant for long—no, it must be felt.

Chapter Eighteen

JULIAN

I told her more than I told my own shrink.

How's that for pathetic?

She was easy to talk to—and I was way past trying to impress someone who was too busy mourning to care if I was a good guy or not—not that I wasn't trying to at least make her understand I wasn't that man anymore, or I tried not to be.

Being a jackass was my default mode.

It protected me.

It kept me safe.

It was the only thing that kept me sane when my dad laughed at me or told me I would never amount to the investment he put into my education and upbringing.

I ran my hands through my hair and leaned against the tile wall of the shower.

I'd needed an escape, not a shower.

Her hands looked like they were healing when I rewrapped them, leaving some fingertips out that seemed undamaged, but I knew I was putting her in danger by not calling someone, so before I flipped on the water, I went outside, called my brother, told him that we needed a car sent up, and then momentarily wanted to take it all back.

I felt desperate.

Like the bubble was about to pop.

It would take a few hours, but they would be here soon.

And this thing between me and Keaton, whatever it was, would end just the way it started, with our cars going in opposite directions, our hearts still sore and healing.

Alone.

It would end with both of us alone.

Loneliness felt like death to me. I'd always had Izzy, I'd always had an end goal, and now I was in limbo, going through the motions and trying to deal with a death I refused to acknowledge.

My own.

The death of the man I used to be and the rebirth of someone who was trying like hell to be better—to be the man my mother had raised.

I pounded my fists against the tile again then flipped off the water and wrapped a towel around my wet body. I was so immersed in my own thoughts that I wasn't watching where I was going when I jerked open the bathroom door and made my way toward the guest bedroom.

Keaton turned a corner.

I stumbled to catch her arms without falling on my ass, and she pressed her hands against my chest as we collided against the wall.

Her hands slid down my wet chest, her stunned expression half hidden by her black hoodie. My blood roared as my heart hammered against my chest, faster and faster the longer she kept her fingers pressed to my skin.

I had promised I wouldn't seduce her.

My body was currently cursing me to hell as her eyes roamed down to the towel that was wrapped around my waist.

She gulped.

If she licked her lips, I was a dead man.

If I saw tongue, I would have no choice but to taste her.

"You—" Her voice was breathless, like she'd been running up and down the halls. "Were dirty?"

I pressed my lips together to keep from smirking. "That's generally why people shower."

"Not the only reason," she teased and took a step back. "Hot or cold?"

"Excuse me?"

"Hot or cold shower?"

I gaped and then narrowed my eyes "If you're suggesting I'm taking cold showers because I told you I'd keep my hands off you and you're just that fucking irresistible that I'm having a hard time keeping my promise . . ." I leaned down and whispered, "You'd be right."

I quickly sidestepped her before I did something that would shatter the cease-fire between us and hurried into my room, shutting the door behind me.

My heart thudded against my chest as I dropped the towel to the floor and walked toward the closet just as a soft knock sounded and the door opened.

I turned, not thinking.

She walked in, eyes lowered to where the towel had just been.

I held my groan in. "Staring doesn't help, Keaton."

"Sorry." Her eyes jerked away. "I, uh, didn't think you would be naked, but it's fine, I can handle naked, I just wondered"—her eyes lowered again, widened—"if . . ."

"If?" I prompted, enjoying the way I distracted her. "Eyes up here, Keaton."

"Sorry!" she snapped. "I just saw something . . . on . . . the wall."

"Something big?"

Her eyes narrowed. "Do you want me to make chocolate chip cook-ies or not?"

"Yes." I nodded.

"Well, good." She crossed her arms. "I'll just be doing it now . . . uh, not *it*, the cookies, not doing the cookies, making—"

"You should go." I grinned.

She rolled her eyes, more at herself than me, it seemed, and left my room so fast the door almost hit her on the way out.

I ignored the release in my chest as I put on a pair of black jeans and a cream sweater.

And realized that several minutes later I was still smiling as I passed the bathroom and walked into the kitchen.

I don't know how long I leaned against the wall and watched her bake. She was actually doing a pretty good job, gauze and all. I'd rewrapped it tighter this time and made sure that a few of her good fingers were exposed on her right hand so that she could do more.

She stared at the mixing bowl and put her hands on her hips then very slowly turned around. "I need your muscle."

I pushed away from the wall. "For homemade cookies, I'd do pretty much anything."

She seemed to perk up. "Really?"

"I feel a question coming."

She frowned. "What makes you say that?"

"You're full of questions." I laughed, grabbed the wooden spoon, and started stirring. "Bet you love puzzles and find extreme enjoyment when each piece fits where it's supposed to. Bet it would drive you batshit crazy if I stole one piece and it was incomplete."

She elbowed me in the side, her closeness giving me a whiff of perfume that had my body aching in all the wrong and right places. "Who would do that?"

"Me. I would do that."

"No cookies for you."

"Hey, the puzzle isn't even real!"

"In my head it is!" she argued with a grin. "Just imagine you're giving the piece back, and I'll let you eat the dough."

I laughed and then paused a few seconds. "Okay, I gave the piece back, and I even left a brand-new puzzle right next to it for you to obsess over. Happy?"

She did a little dance. "Best imaginary gift anyone has ever given me."

"I live to please," I said dryly, stirring the ingredients with fervor while she bent over to grab a cookie sheet.

I stepped back so I wouldn't run into her, and when she flipped around she nearly collided with the bowl. I caught her by the arms and held her still. "Is this your new thing? Colliding with me?"

"Is this your new thing?" Her breath came out in a short exhale. "Manhandling me?"

I grinned down at her. "Oh, princess, you'd know if I was manhandling you . . ."

Her eyes dilated before she jerked away and laughed. "Yeah, well, I'm more of a nonaggressive sort of . . . person."

"Hmm." I went back to the bowl and started making small balls with my hands. "Your words don't match your eyes."

"What's that supposed to mean?" She turned on the oven and grabbed another cookie sheet, not looking at me.

"It's not appropriate talk during cookie making, the chocolate chips might hear."

She snorted out a laugh. "I can take it, so can they. Try me, I'm game . . ."

I dropped the dough and trapped her against the counter, a hand on either side of her body while mine pressed into hers. "America's sweetheart doesn't always want sweet, that's what I think." I traced a finger down her chin while she licked her lips. "I think a part of you wants to be wild, and I think that you've yet to experience it."

Her nostrils flared. "That's not fair."

"I didn't say it was," I said softly. "I'm just saying you don't have to pretend, not around me. Trust me, I'm not worth the façade." I dropped my hands and returned to the dough.

"You're wrong." Her voice came a few seconds later. "I'm not pretending, you know . . . I'm just protecting myself . . ."

"From what?"

She gulped, and then guilt flashed across her face as she whispered, "You."

In all my years of living, one word has never had such a precise impact as it twisted its way toward my heart and hit its mark.

Noah had been her savior.

And she saw me as her downfall.

"I'm . . ." I wasn't sure why the truth hurt. I never lied to her about the sort of man I was, but I thought that maybe she saw me as more than that. I thought she saw me as the man I was trying to be. I was rarely wrong about people, but I guess in this case . . . "I'm really tired . . . I'm going to go to sleep."

"Julian—"

"No, it's fine . . ." I forced a smile. "Help should be here in the next few hours anyway, at least by morning."

"What?" Her face paled. "What do you mean?"

"I mean I called in help, so that you don't die from an infection."

"When did you get cell reception?"

I cursed. "A while ago."

"Why is it taking so long then if it was a while ago?"

"Because I'm exactly who you think I am," I admitted. "A selfish bastard who wanted more time with a pretty girl because he thought she saw more than everyone else. Stupid, I know. I called before my shower. Enjoy the cookies."

I left.

I didn't want to see the guilt on her face.

I didn't want her to see the sadness on mine.

A rational part of me told me I was being unfair, we barely knew each other.

But the other part, the part that hoped and dreamed, the part that was hungry for a real connection—told me that she was different, this would be different. It told me to hold on to this moment because it was a rare one.

Unfortunately, she didn't feel the same way.

I made my way back to my bedroom and flipped off the lights, then lay down and stared wide-eyed at the ceiling.

Chapter Nineteen

I regretted my words instantly.

The fact was, Julian made me feel a lot of things: guilt, attraction, fascination. And it wasn't fair to him that as much as I wanted to reach out and touch him, I also wanted to pull away and crawl into myself.

It wasn't fair.

But it was happening.

The fact that he seemed to have delayed calling for help only momentarily upset me. My hands were feeling better, obviously, and in his own way, it was sweet that he wanted to keep us isolated a bit longer.

I leaned against the counter as the oven dinged. The smell of fresh cookies filled the air. Guilt slammed into my chest as I grabbed a plate and started shoveling the mountain of cookies onto it in order to bring Julian a peace offering.

His eyes.

I shivered.

He'd closed me off in seconds.

I wondered if that was how he dealt with pain. He just decided it hurt too much and refused to feel it, moved right along and shoved it in the back of his mind. It seemed he was talented at deflecting, ignoring, pretending.

I didn't like it.

I liked it when he was open.

When he laughed, when he shared.

Did he do that with his ex?

Why was I even thinking about her?

Because she'd obviously been amazing enough to be his.

And I was stupidly curious and admittedly jealous.

With a sigh, I grabbed the plate and stared at the computer. It would all be over in a few hours, wouldn't it? Him helping me with my story. Me talking about Noah.

It felt like my throat was closing up.

How was I going to do this without Julian?

And how had he helped so much in the last forty-eight hours? He let me talk about the sad, the happy, the real and was quiet the entire time except for the tapping of his fingers against the keys.

I gripped the heavy plate and made my way down the hall to his bedroom. I didn't knock, I didn't want to wake him up. I just wanted him to smell the cookies and enjoy them once he was done sleeping.

I twisted the handle to the door and let myself in, leaving it open a crack for my quick escape.

He was sprawled across the large king bed, shirtless.

I quickly looked away and set the cookies on the nightstand and stole one more look at him before backing away.

"Is that a peace offering?" His groggy voice startled me.

I shivered, and crossed my arms. "Yeah, well, you gave the puzzle piece back, so it's only fair, right?"

"Right," he agreed.

The silence was tense.

I wasn't sure if I should ask if he was okay, apologize, or just leave.

"If I ask you something, will you promise not to read into it?" he finally said.

I took a step toward him. "Sure."

"Stay."

"Is that the question?" I felt all the air leave my lungs.

"More or less," he said. "Just stay. Please?"

"Afraid of the dark?" I teased as I slowly climbed into the bed and lay down next to him.

I didn't pull away when his hand softly clasped my right bandaged one and lightly squeezed. "The night is dark and full of terrors."

"*Game of Thrones.*"

"I knew I liked you."

I squeezed his hand back as best I could. "Why am I lying in your bed, Julian?"

"Because I did the math. Born with a spreadsheet in my hands, remember? They'll be here in about three hours, and I'm a horrible enough human being to do anything in my power to keep you with me for just a little bit longer."

"Why?" What I meant to say was *Why me*, but I couldn't get the words out.

"Because . . ." He sighed and wrapped an arm around me, pulling me close. "When I touch you, I don't feel so alone."

"Me either."

"Sleep."

Sleep? He was insane. His body was searing hot, he had no shirt on, and he was calmly holding me in bed like it was a natural occurrence for me, for us.

My body was hypersensitive to his every breath, even the slowing of it telling me he was sleeping.

I forced myself to relax and ducked my head against his chest. The last thing I remembered was the smell of cologne and chocolate chip cookies.

It was the first time in months I fell asleep with a smile on my face and less heaviness in my heart.

Chapter Twenty

JULIAN

It wasn't the smell of cookies that woke me up out of a dead sleep. It was a mouth breathing below my right ear, lips pressed against my skin like they belonged there.

I exhaled slowly and told myself not to react.

She was sleeping.

I wanted her close.

It meant nothing.

She'd brought cookies.

End of story.

I was afraid to move too much, but I wanted to check the time. It was even darker now, meaning we would have company soon, invited company that I wanted to send packing.

I turned my head slightly as Keaton clung tighter to me.

I felt a pull so strong that it made my chest tight, a pull to her. Something tethered us, and I had no idea what it was. Maybe it was just the pain we both carried around us like a protective armor, but I had to wonder if my tumultuous emotions were anything like Bridge's when he stole what was mine.

When he lay next to my fiancée and kissed her mouth.

Did the guilt rival that pull?

It would have had to.

Because I felt like I was in a situation I couldn't win. I couldn't compete with a guy who was dead—I knew I wouldn't win against him, that I didn't stand a chance, and yet the feeling was still there.

And it was taking every ounce of control I had not to act on it, throw caution to the wind, and lie to myself and her that it would just be scratching an itch, getting it out of our systems.

I highly doubted she was someone you ever got over.

Once Keaton was in you . . .

You were damned.

I would drown in her and never be the same. I was already struggling with leaving her, with walking in the opposite direction while she finished her book, returned to her family and friends, her life.

While I returned to an empty apartment.

My expensive cars.

Lavish lifestyle.

And absolutely nobody to share it with.

Keaton made a noise. I opened my mouth to ask her if she was okay when she nuzzled my neck again.

Damn it, I wasn't a saint.

Never claimed to be.

Izzy and Bridge could easily attest to that.

I gritted my teeth while she moaned in her sleep, and tried to think about anything but the fact that her soft body was rubbing up against mine.

Be a gentleman.

Keep your clothes on.

I clutched the sheet with my left hand and squeezed my eyes shut while a leg made its way over my body, pinning me to the bed.

I was going to die in a pool of my own sweat and good intentions, wasn't I? She made another little noise of contentment.

Glad one of us was happy and not dying a slow, sweaty death.

I tried moving away from her, slowly peeling my body from hers, but her leg hooked itself around me, and the last thing I wanted to do was wake her up. She would be embarrassed, and then she would see I was uncomfortable in more ways than one and she'd probably slap me.

I would deserve it.

Not that it mattered.

Just when I was ready to move my arm again, or attempt to, she jerked away and lifted her head, nearly knocking it against mine.

I cursed. "Who the hell wakes up like that?"

She squinted her eyes. "Why are you watching me sleep?"

"I wasn't!" I said defensively. "I was sleeping and woke up being suffocated by your body and was trying to escape."

"Escape?" She frowned and then looked down. "Oh, sorry, I'm an extremely violent sleeper."

"And you don't think that would have been a good thing to lead with when I asked you to lie down?"

Her eyes narrowed, she looked fierce and cute all at once. Damn it. "I was doing you a favor!"

"Why are you yelling?"

"I don't know!" She pouted. "I was having a really good dream."

I shot her a smug grin. "What kind of dream? You were doing an awful lot of moaning . . ."

She scowled. "It wasn't . . . not like, I mean there was no sex, just . . . touching."

"Who was touching you?"

"Nobody," she snapped.

I grinned so wide my face hurt. "Princess, were you dreaming about me?"

"You wish."

"Good comeback."

Another scowl. "Dreams are merely the brain's way of processing the things that happen to us throughout the day. You kissed me, and apparently my brain needed to sort that into a box that made sense."

"Hmm, where did your brain put me? Because if I'm not in the best-kiss-of-my-life box, I'm going to have to ask for a second opinion."

She laughed at that. "You have an extremely high opinion of your own kissing skills."

"A well-earned high opinion," I added helpfully, not realizing I was reaching for her until it was too late, until my fingertips were stroking her hair and tucking it behind her ear, until I noticed her light gasp at my touch and the way she focused on my mouth like I was tastier than the cookies on the nightstand. "You can't look at me like that, princess, I'm not known for my extreme self-control . . ."

"And yet you've been doing so well."

"Cold showers," I joked.

Which just made her duck her head and laugh against my neck. "Why are you so easy?"

"I think I'm offended," I grumbled, leaning back against the pillow while she joined me, placing her gauzed-up hand on my chest and drawing small circles.

"You know what I mean. It's only been a few days. Normally I'd be bolting my door closed, sleeping with a knife under my pillow."

"Dear God, please tell me you didn't bring the knife in here."

"No." She laughed. "It's safe in the kitchen."

"Not what I'd call safe since you can still access it, but I'll take what I can get." My mind and heart raced like crazy. Time continued to slip right by us, and it didn't seem like we were going to have enough to hash out whatever was taking place between us.

Because as crazy as it sounded.

She was right.

It was easy with her.

It was like finding someone and immediately having inside jokes, reading their mind and knowing their thoughts without even trying. It wasn't something I'd ever experienced or hoped to experience once Izzy chose Bridge.

"What happens tomorrow? What happens in a few hours?" Keaton asked softly like she wanted—no, *needed* me to tell her something good, something happy.

I let out a long sigh. "That's the beauty of being the one who's living, Keaton. You get to decide how you spend each moment you're given."

"There are always consequences."

I just shrugged. "I'm done being that person, the one who measures everything by what could happen or what should. It's exhausting, and there's nothing like being brought back from near death to show you how important it is to do something with the seconds you have even if they don't amount to the same as others you've lost."

"Okay." She nodded her head; I felt it against my chest. "You know, for being a rich man whore, you're pretty wise."

I smiled. "I have my moments."

"You have more than that, Julian." She said it like she had full confidence in my ability to make good life decisions, when all I really wanted to do in that moment was kiss her, breathe her in, strip her down, and lose myself in her.

"Do you want a cookie?" she asked in a lazy voice.

I frowned at the subject change. "I guess since someone woke me up . . ."

She moved to grab a cookie from the nightstand, then fell back against my chest. I loved her there. Keaton dangled the treat in front of my lips.

I took one huge bite and moaned. "You should probably move in with me."

"And just make you cookies every day?"

I felt my eyes heat while I watched her watch me. "Yeah . . . just cookies."

"Liar." She looked away and bit down on the cookie. A piece of chocolate stuck to her lower lip. I reached up and brushed it away.

Her body shuddered as she closed her eyes and leaned toward me. "Did you get all of it?"

I pressed my fingertips against the cookie in her hand, swiped some melted chocolate onto my finger and then brushed it against her lower lip and whispered, "No."

"Well?" She opened her eyes.

I cupped the back of her head and leaned in, brushing my lips across hers before licking her bottom lip and pulling away. "Got it."

She shook her head no and leaned forward, crushing her mouth against mine in a way that was as aggressive as I'd wanted to kiss her. Punishing, bruising, sad mixed with a heavy amount of ache.

Our pain collided with that kiss.

And like setting fire to gasoline.

We were ignited whole.

I wrapped my arms around her, lifting her onto my body while she straddled me. Cookie abandoned, her hands gently cupped my head as I grabbed her shirt, jerked it over her body, and threw it to the ground, briefly breaking the kiss while her hands flew to my jeans.

She fumbled with the first button. I grinned against her mouth. "Having trouble?"

"Injured," she said between kisses. "What are we doing?"

"Stop thinking." I kissed her hard then, so hard that it consumed me, set me on fire, set my heart hammering in a chaotic rhythm that refused to let up. I undid the buttons and kicked the jeans down while she moved off me and lay down on her back.

I wasn't prepared for the vision of her hair spread out across my pillow, or the way her lips looked swollen and pink from our kiss. I leaned over her and gently pulled the sweats she was wearing down her legs, leaving her in neon-pink underwear and black bra with all the polka dots. "We really need to talk about your lingerie."

She laughed and kissed me again. "Because you love it so much?"

"I'm going to go blind from all the neon polka dots." I laughed, and then nearly stopped kissing her. We were laughing, half naked, more than likely going to have sex . . . and we were talking, conversing.

Why was it so easy?

"You said to stop thinking." She brought my attention back to her. I was insane to even look away from her eyes.

"I don't feel like we have enough time," I admitted. "Not for what I want to do to you, not for the things I want to make you feel." I traced my tongue across her lower lip and bit down on it as my hands spread across her breasts. She arched off the bed with each graze of my fingertips. "I would spend hours right *here*."

"We don't have hours." She sounded as sad as I felt.

"No."

We were never meant to be.

She was meant for him.

And I had been meant for someone else.

Maybe the universe was playing a sick joke on us to bring us together when we needed it the most, when we were at our most vulnerable, only for the harsh reality of our circumstances to settle in.

Different worlds.

Both in the limelight.

But it could work.

Right?

I kissed her harder and braced her hips with my hands while she twisted her tongue around mine. She tasted like chocolate. Our breath mingled, joined, and I pulled down her pink underwear and cupped her ass. Her skin was smooth against my fingertips as I moved my hand between her thighs.

"Julian." She whispered my name like she knew how much it meant to be wanted, to be needed. "You're wasting time."

"This," I said and moved my fingers, "is never a waste."

"Oh." She squeezed her eyes shut. "I know nothing, keep going, I'll just lie here."

"You say that like you're still," I joked and teased her entrance more while tremors wracked her body.

"Born with a spreadsheet in one hand and extreme talent in the other," she said under her breath, making a grin spread across my face as she came off the bed and nearly head-butted me.

"Not just a violent sleeper, then," I teased, pulling her to her knees and kissing her across the mouth, angling a different way to get more of her. I wanted to take it all.

"Hmm, no," she answered, wrapping her arms around my neck. "I don't do this."

"Do what?" I pulled away from her despite the fact that my body was ready to explode.

"This." She gulped. "I don't do one-night stands."

"Who says it's just one night?" I did it; I put myself out there on the ledge.

Her eyes lit up a bit, and then she looked away.

"Stay with me, Keaton."

A small nod and then she was kissing me again, testing my strength, my patience, as I pushed her onto her back and thrust into her with one smooth movement.

Her skin was dipped in moonlight, her eyes full of wonder as she clung to me and strained up like she needed more than just our bodies to be linked but also our mouths.

I slowed down my movements and kissed her hard and deep, while her heat held me prisoner, pulsed around me in a way that was damn near magical.

I couldn't imagine ever looking back on this moment and having a regret, not with Keaton, never with Keaton.

This was different.

We were different.

This was no one-night stand.

This was the beginning.

Just like the book.

The beginning of us.

She broke off the kiss. "This feels . . . incredible, you feel . . ."

Right. She felt so fucking right.

The only thing that had felt right in the last four months was making love to Keaton Westbrook, kissing her, licking chocolate off her face, playing cards.

The only right thing.

I pumped into her again and again, as my body drew up, tightened, begged for release.

I would have sold my entire fortune for that moment to last forever.

I would have given up every fancy car, every suit, every stock.

To spend more time with her in my arms.

She yelled my name.

And I whispered hers reverently in return as I kissed down her neck and felt her release like it was my own. I felt every tremor of her thighs, every rough exhale as she came down from the feeling of flying and found gravity again.

It was too easy to follow her.

To let my feelings claim a protective ownership of her and what we could possibly have.

I chased after her, I kissed her harder and found my release, and I was actually afraid to open my eyes when I moved away from her, out of breath as we both stared up at the ceiling, completely naked, sweaty, sated.

"So . . ." Keaton's voice cracked. "Did you want another cookie?"

I burst out laughing. "I can't decide if you really mean that or if it's code for something else."

She leaned up on her elbow and smiled down at me. "Can't it be both?"

Hell yeah, it could.

I moved to kiss her at about the same time a bright light streamed through the window followed by the sound of a helicopter and Keaton pulling away in a rush to get her clothes on, all the while cursing some guy named Gene to hell.

Chapter Twenty-One

KEATON

I had no time to process the fact that I'd just slept with Julian, less than a year after laying my boyfriend to rest, mere months after saying goodbye. We'd had a complicated relationship, we were physical in the beginning, not so much in the end.

Not so much at all.

I tamped down my feelings, attempted to get my shirt on the right way, and jerked open the door at about the same time someone tried shoving it open.

Someone who wasn't Gene.

But an exact replica of Julian.

The only difference was their hair.

Julian's was longer, this guy—Bridge, I believed his name was—had it cut a bit shorter and messier. It also wasn't as glossy as Julian's, not that I was comparing them.

Maybe I was.

At his side was a beautiful woman with sharp features and crystal-green eyes. She was wearing a gorgeous pair of leather leggings, a fake-fur coat, and thigh-high boots that looked really out of place in the snow.

"Hi," I said dumbly.

"Did you guys really need to bring the helicopter?" Julian's lazy voice came from behind me. I turned around and felt my entire body heat and blush simultaneously. You would have to be dumb as a rock not to know what we had just been doing.

The cabin smelled like sweaty sex and chocolate chip cookies.

I kept a smile pasted on my face when all I wanted to do was escape, especially because Izzy, Julian's ex, kept inspecting me like she was trying to place who I was or what I was doing there.

"KEATON WESTBROOK!" she finally yelled, making me jump a foot and nearly collide with Bridge. "I KNEW I recognized you!"

"Yeah." I smiled shyly. "Live and in person."

"I just read an article about all of your amazing work with the children's cancer hospital in Manhattan! I volunteer on a different wing, but you're incredible. I'm so sorry for your loss." She was being sincere.

I knew that.

But I'd just slept with Julian.

It was too raw.

Everything.

What the hell did I just do?

Noah would be so disappointed in me.

I was disappointed in me.

I'd just hopped into bed with a relative stranger because he made me feel good. I wasn't that girl, had never been that girl.

I felt the tears again, and I smiled harder to keep them in while Izzy pulled me in for a hug. "I would love to take you out. I do a lot of charity work with—"

"Iz . . ." Bridge interrupted her. "Let's maybe get them out of the cabin before you start plotting world domination."

I almost threw him a parade. His eyes narrowed in on me and then his smile was back in place as he made his way over to Julian and pulled him in for a hug that looked painful to watch.

Julian still hadn't forgiven him; that much was extremely clear.

And yet he'd slept with me.

Had we used each other?

Or was it more?

I crossed my arms. "Um, it's going to take us a while to pack up everything—"

"Don't worry about that," Bridge said with a shrug. "I have a crew coming up here tomorrow to clear the roads for the other tenants in the area. They'll grab all your stuff and deliver it to wherever it needs to go. Besides, we need to get you to a doctor. Julian said you got frostbite and fought off an elk all by yourself."

I smiled at that. "Julian exaggerates, but had he not found me, I would have most likely been an icicle, frozen facedown in the snow."

Izzy put her hand over her mouth. "What were you doing outside?"

"Oh, you know, trying to appease the master of the cabin and build another fire . . ." I glared playfully at Julian, who just smiled and looked down.

Bridge narrowed his eyes at me then at Julian as a small smile spread across his mouth. "Uh-huh, alright. That's the story you guys are going to go with?"

"Yup," we said in unison, earning a chuckle from Bridge and Izzy.

The days spent with Julian had been slow, enjoyable, like sitting by a campfire and living in the moment.

And then suddenly, I had my laptop and one of my duffel bags, and I was in a helicopter sitting next to him, wondering how it all happened so fast, the rescue, the fact that I could already see the city lights.

We landed at one of the private airports near Brooklyn, where an ambulance was already waiting.

I frowned and pointed. "That's not necessary."

Bridge snorted. "Tell that to my brother."

"I'm fine," I said, only to get ignored by Julian, who helped me out of the helicopter and into the waiting ambulance, where an EMT began to unwrap my hands. "Seriously, I'll be okay."

"Hold still, ma'am, have you had any tingling sensations? A fever?" He started firing off questions while Julian stood there.

I don't remember answering.

All I could focus on was Julian's face, his expression expectant.

Like he was waiting for something.

Another moment, maybe.

My mouth felt dry. I wanted to ask him to stay, I wanted to tell him that it was too soon, but I didn't know how. He was Julian Tennyson. Did he even care?

The wind picked up, and still he stood there, hands in the pocket of the jeans I'd helped take off, expression hopeful.

"Let's go." The EMT hit the roof of the ambulance and closed one door.

And still I said nothing.

I still had time.

I opened my mouth and all that came out was "Thank you."

And I knew, though I had somehow survived Noah's death, I would never get over the expression of rejection on Julian's face as the second door closed.

Never.

Chapter Twenty-Two

Waking up from a coma only to find out that everything has been taken from you . . . sucks.

It's painful, both physically and emotionally.

But watching that ambulance drive off rivaled that feeling and then trumped it when I finally walked into my brand-new penthouse apartment that overlooked the city.

Alone.

No chocolate chip cookies.

No roaring fireplace in the corner.

No laptop keys to hit.

Just nothingness.

I didn't even get her phone number.

I should have asked.

I was going to, but then she just gave me this look of . . . no. I couldn't explain it, but I wanted her to be ready, I wanted her to be excited, to say something, anything.

I wasn't stupid, I knew that I never fought for Izzy, but I never thought in my wildest dreams that the next girl I fell for would refuse to fight for me.

It didn't just sting my pride.

It hurt my heart in a way I wasn't prepared for, stole the air from my lungs, making it impossible to breathe normally.

I grabbed a bottle of Maker's Mark and sat in my living room.

In the dark.

And poured.

And when the doorbell rang, I nearly knocked over my drink in anticipation of seeing her, only to realize halfway to the door that she didn't know where I lived, and if she didn't want me with her in the ambulance, she sure as hell wasn't going to seek me out and show up on my doorstep.

Fuck, I could still smell her on my skin.

Taste her on my lips.

I pulled the door open to find Bridge giving me a knowing look before lifting a bottle of expensive whiskey and saying, "So, Keaton Westbrook?"

I almost slammed the door in his face.

Except I had no one else.

Literally.

And I was that low.

So I hung my head, let him in, grabbed the whiskey, popped the cork, took a giant swig, and muttered, "I like her."

Bridge was quiet, and then he burst out laughing. "Well, did she write you a note back, or are you still waiting for her to circle yes or no?"

"Jackass." I shoved him. "I didn't come right out and say it. She was dealing with things, and you know how I've been. I just . . . it doesn't matter. I'm still technically on vacation, maybe I'll go to Colorado or something . . ."

"Bullshit, you aren't going anywhere, especially if she's here in the city."

He was right about that, I needed a distraction so I didn't end up at her doorstep drunk off my ass. "You think they'll let me come back to work early?"

"That would be a no," Bridge said immediately. "But you do have a few weeks to get your stalker skills on. She's not going back to LA until later this year. She goes between both cities, just in case you weren't aware, and I wish I wasn't aware, but apparently Izzy follows her on Instagram."

I almost threw myself against a blunt object. "Of course she does."

"You wanna talk about it?"

I stared into the bottle of brown liquid wondering how much alcohol it would take to numb the space between my ribs that wouldn't stop hurting. "Talking won't make it better."

"Make what better? Because the way I see it, we arrived to save a day that didn't really need saving. Your hair was a mess, her mouth was swollen, color high. Oh, and you had only pants on and looked way too happy to see me. The last time you smiled at me like that was never, so what happened?"

I let out a rough exhale and ran my fingers through my hair. "I'm a hopeful idiot, that's what happened."

"Hopeful?"

"We had sex."

"NO!"

"I'm seconds away from shoving you out my window, you've been warned."

He grinned. "I figured as much, the entire house was like this cozy little—" He stopped when I shot him a glare. "So what's the plan? Are you going to call her?"

"I don't have her number."

"Why?"

"Because it never came up? Because maybe to her it was a one-time thing? Because she just buried her boyfriend less than a year ago, and I'm not stupid enough to think I could compete against a dead guy when I couldn't even keep my own fiancée away from my brother. I don't know, Bridge, you tell me!" I didn't realize I was pacing until I looked down. Shit. I took another swig straight from the bottle and waited for him to say something.

What came out wasn't what I expected. "You're different, Julian. Everyone knows that. You're . . . not the same guy."

"This conversation, not making me feel better, Bridge."

"You know what I mean." He stood. "The coma changed you, you work your ass off, you rarely go out, you've bailed on every company event, including the gala. You do two things: go to the gym and work, and then sometimes when you're feeling crazy you go to the gym twice in one day."

"I'm trying to get bigger than you so when I do kick your ass it hurts." I glared over the bottle.

He rolled his eyes. "I already told you that I'd gladly let you throw punches if you'd just react to something—anything. You're alive, but you're not living, man, you may as well have died with Mom."

I charged him, bottle in hand. "Take it back!"

"No." He eyed me up and down. "I won't."

"Son of a bitch." I clenched my teeth and set the bottle down, then collapsed onto the couch. "Why are you here again?"

"Well, I was here to make sure you were okay and bring you your favorite whiskey, and then when I saw you drinking alone I got concerned, especially since you seemed actually happy at the cabin . . . with her."

I swallowed slowly. "I was."

"Then that's your answer." He said it like it was so simple. "Seek her out, get her number, take her to lunch, live a little."

I nodded. "Maybe."

"Fight for what you want, Julian."

"Like I didn't fight for Izzy? Is that what you mean?"

"Don't put words into my mouth. You fought for her the only way you knew how, by fighting our father in order to protect her, to protect all of us. Let it go and move on. You deserve it."

Then why didn't I feel like it?

Why did I feel so defeated and like I didn't stand a chance?

I shrugged, earning another sigh from Bridge as he walked toward the door then called over his shoulder, "You know you could always just slide into her DMs."

"The fact that you just uttered that sentence makes me want to go back in time and prevent the universe from creating it." I laughed. "You don't just slide into a girl's DMs on Instagram, that's like sending a dick pic."

"Even better!" Bridge agreed. "That's the spirit, show her what she's missing."

"How am I the one dying alone?" I wondered out loud.

Bridge opened the door and wiggled his eyebrows at me. "Stop feeling sorry for yourself, man up with some of that Tennyson grit, and go troll her social media."

I stared him down. "I can't decide if this is the best pep talk or the absolute worst."

He winked and shut the door behind him.

And I stupidly took his advice, grabbed my phone, and immediately started following her on Instagram.

Along with seventeen and a half million other fans.

Great advice, Bridge. Great.

Defeated, I tossed my phone against the couch and went in search of clean clothes.

Chapter Twenty-Three

KEATON

My hands would heal.

I wasn't going to lose any digits.

And I was no longer trapped by a killer elk and three feet of snow.

And I was sad.

I told my parents not to fly in and sent them a nice little proof-of-life photo. I filled them in on the need-to-know details and told them I was camping out in their lavish apartment until I figured out my next move.

The only problem?

He was in the city.

And because of that, I found that I didn't want to leave.

To make matters worse, the words were gone.

I stared at my laptop the very next day with a fresh cup of coffee in my hand and a strong feeling that everything was going to be okay. I just had to tell the story.

Except, the minute I started typing, I wasn't thinking of Noah. I was thinking about Julian.

About his mouth.

The way he kissed me.

Every all-consuming smile he flashed my way, the teasing, and the look on his face when the ambulance pulled away.

I didn't have his phone number, I hadn't even thought about it. And now I felt weird just randomly looking him up and going, *"Oh hey, remember me? The girl who coerced you into sex after chocolate chip cookies?"*

I frowned at the laptop screen.

I hadn't exactly coerced him.

It had been a joint decision, right?

I thought back about the hesitation in his eyes, the way he licked the chocolate from my lips and waited like he needed permission from me, and the embarrassing way I basically threw myself at him with wild abandon.

I squeezed my eyes shut and shook my head. It would be fine. I was alone in my parents' Manhattan penthouse, and all I kept thinking was how I missed the cabin.

But I missed Julian more.

I put my hands on the keyboard and took a deep breath, just as my cell started to buzz.

Thank. God.

I didn't recognize the number, but took it as a sign from the universe and quickly said, "Hello?"

"Keaton?" The feminine voice sounded familiar. "Keaton Westbrook?"

Great, another fan found my number. I was going to have to change it again. "Yeah, that's me," I said with fake excitement.

"Oh, good! Your publicist said this was the right one, but I wasn't sure since she said you've had to change your number so many times. Anyways, I was calling to see if you'd like to go to the surprise party."

"Surprise party," I repeated like a parrot. "I'm sorry, who is this?"

"Oh God, I'm such an idiot. In my head I already told you. Ugh, pregnancy brain. This is Izzy Tennyson."

My mouth went completely dry. "Oh, h-hey there." I gulped and squeezed my eyes shut.

She laughed. "So the party is next Friday, they rented out the entire Met for Bridge and Julian's birthday. It's going to be incredible, and neither of them knows it's happening, mainly because they'd both bail and get drunk in a closet somewhere rather than show up, and we can't have that. Please say you'll come!"

"Um . . ."

"It would mean a lot to Julian," she said softly, apparently pulling out the big guns. "He was forced to take some time off, you know . . . at least three weeks. He's going to be a grumpy bear, and it might be nice to have someone he likes there so he doesn't scare everyone away."

"He has you." I said it without thinking.

She was silent and then, "Hard to believe, since we were friends first, but I'm not Julian's favorite person, and I refuse to force forgiveness where it's not earned. I deserve it, I made the choice, not Bridge, not Julian, but me. When love finds you, true love, it doesn't give you the chance to say no, and you realize that you would rather suffer the rest of your life with your decisions than suffer without it."

I sighed. Well, when she put it that way. "I'll be there."

"Great!" I could practically feel her beaming through the phone. "I'll get the rest of the details over to your publicist. It's a gala, so obviously wear a gown. If you want to know the designers that are helping sponsor the event, I can let you know so you can wear one of their pieces, or wear whatever you want, but I know since it's you they'd jump at the opportunity to dress you."

I smiled at that. "How about you pair me up with the designer who needs the publicity the most?"

She was silent.

I waited.

"Izzy?"

She sniffed. "Sorry, I'm so hormonal. That's really sweet, I knew I liked you. You're perfect for him."

I didn't know what to say, so I just said, "Thank you. I'll see you next week."

"Can't wait!"

She hung up.

And I stared at my computer and quickly wrote down what I was thinking.

Noah was my first love.

He was someone who made me think about the world differently.

Noah was my world.

Cancer consumed him the way he consumed me.

After our first date, we were inseparable. He entertained me with stories about his childhood, and the second day we were together, he told me he was going to kiss me.

His kiss felt unlike any kiss I'd ever had.

Until two days ago, when Julian Tennyson kissed me and stole the only fragment of my still-beating heart.

Love doesn't always end with death. Sometimes, that's where it takes root.

I was happy with what I had written, but a part of me was still conflicted, like I was writing a story that should be written with Julian. It was ridiculous. I snapped a picture and posted to Instagram, knowing that my fans would be excited. I was just about to close out the app when I noticed several hundred new comments on one of my last posts.

It was a picture of me sitting by myself smiling into a cup of coffee. The caption talked about moving on with life even though it's difficult.

The comments, however, were scathing.

It seemed everyone was there for me when Noah was struggling, but even hinting at moving on had set people off. Comments about cheating, and it being too soon, and calling me a whore.

My stomach dropped.

I quickly set my phone down and tried to suck in some air. Why hadn't my team told me about this?

I felt nauseated as I paced the apartment. It was like going through Noah's struggle all over again as panic seized my lungs. I started hyperventilating and quickly moved to the kitchen to grab a paper bag.

I tried breathing into it so I wouldn't pass out, then went in search of the Xanax my doctor had prescribed for my panic attacks.

They'd started when we were told Noah's treatments weren't working.

I'd had a horrible nightmare that he'd died in my arms while we were sleeping and that I never got to say goodbye.

It was always harder at night.

And rationally I knew that there was nothing different at night, just the absence of light, but for some reason that absence just reminded me that he was gone and that I was all alone, living without him.

I popped a small pill, but it did nothing to ease the anxiety twisting my stomach into knots—because if they knew about Julian, the brand that I'd built would be in jeopardy and even more so, it would impact the book.

The one thing I had promised to do.

Write our story.

And it could all go up in flames with one social media post holding Julian's hand.

It wasn't fair.

To either of us.

Then again, it wasn't like it was going to go beyond just that one time, right? I gulped. The problem was that I liked him, I liked his raw honesty, his sensitivity, and the way that he made me feel when I talked about Noah. He didn't cut me off or start talking about himself; he was eerily quiet and made me think he wanted to know more.

But we weren't in the cabin anymore, secluded away from the real world. I mentally prepared myself for all of the media at his surprise party. I'd thank him for his help at the cabin and I'd move on.

I would not repeat the same mistake of leaning into his cologne or letting my heart slam against my chest every time he smiled at me.

I'd say happy birthday, and I'd bolt.

Perfect plan.

If only I had confidence that I could stick to it without falling for his lethal charms.

Chapter Twenty-Four

JULIAN

The city was always my favorite place at night, something about the lights made me feel alive even when I was in a bad mood and bored out of my mind. And not just that, but torturing myself with images and memories of my night with Keaton, like reliving it in my head was going to be anything like the real thing. The car pulled up to another stoplight. I was probably going to be late, and I really didn't care.

If I had it my way, I'd make an appearance, shake hands, drink one glass of champagne, then go back to my apartment and creep Keaton's Instagram like I'd been doing for the past week and a half.

I'd yet to grow a pair of balls and message Keaton, but I'd done a really good job of looking over every single picture she posted like a madman, and when I came to the pictures of her and Noah, some sick curiosity took over.

My forced vacation was turning me into a stalker.

And not even a really good one.

We'd gotten back into the city late on a Wednesday, it was already a week and a half later, and all I'd done was convinced myself that Noah was superhuman and that no man would ever compare to him.

Literally.

I wasn't even exaggerating; that's the caption she wrote beneath the last photo of them a year ago.

I was driving myself crazy.

Hadn't done anything except work out and watch TV, and Bridge wouldn't stop calling me to remind me about the business dinner I was en route to.

I didn't even bother with a tie.

I almost laughed, I didn't even recognize myself anymore. Last year I wouldn't have been caught dead going to a business dinner without running a lint roller over my suit, and today I'd gotten ready in ten minutes and called it good.

When the car pulled up to the curb, I realized that was most likely a grievous error on my part.

Paparazzi lined a red carpet leading to the stairs and all the way up into the entrance, and hanging from the building was a banner with the largest picture of my face I had ever seen. Seriously, billboard-sized.

Scrawled between our two photos, in letters probably ten feet tall, was *Happy Birthday, Julian and Bridge!*

I was killing Izzy.

This had her written all over it.

I gritted my teeth until my jaw hurt and ran my hands through my hair before the door opened and, like an out-of-body experience, like walking through mud, I slowly made my way up the stairs amidst screams from the media.

"Is it true you cheated on your fiancée and she left you for your brother?"

"Are you gay?"

"Did someone murder your mother?"

"Julian, are you still on drugs?" *Seriously?*

"Your father said you have a drinking problem . . ." Oh good, let's talk about him on my birthday.

My plan had been to celebrate with a quiet dinner at the apartment followed by Jimmy Fallon.

God, I was a mess.

I forced a smile I didn't feel as cameras flashed and more questions were fired toward me. I felt old, so old in that moment, older than my thirty-two years as I finally made it to the top of the stairs to see Izzy waving wildly at me. She was in a sleek black dress that hugged every curve, including her rapidly growing stomach.

A baby.

His baby. Not mine.

My ex-fiancée.

I almost turned around and bolted.

Would I ever get used to it?

To them?

I was already exhausted, and the night had just started. "Izzy, I take it this is all you?" I leaned in and pressed a kiss to each cheek.

She didn't let me get away without a hug.

Ever since the beginning of her pregnancy she'd been emotional. She'd even called me, bawling and apologizing—yet again—for everything during the coma.

I told her I forgave her.

And I did.

But that didn't mean it was easy to hug her then return her to my brother.

"Bridge." I shook his hand.

He too pulled me in for a hug, then whispered in my ear, "They locked all exits, I checked."

I laughed. "She actually let you out of her sight?"

He glared. "I can be stealthy."

Izzy rolled her eyes. "Easily defeated, both of you. Now, go inside, sip some champagne and—" Her eyes lit up. "Actually don't go inside. Julian, count to three and turn around."

"Izzy, swear to me you didn't get a giant cake with a person in it."
I groaned.

Bridge's eyebrows shot up. "Not a giant cake."

Izzy beamed. "Before you get mad at me for meddling . . . know that I didn't even have to convince her."

"Her?"

"Three seconds is over, bro." Bridge grinned just as someone tapped me on the shoulder.

Slowly I turned, and then I nearly had a heart attack on the stairs.

"Keaton." Stunned, I gaped at her as though I'd never seen an attractive woman before. Her golden hair cascaded in loose waves around her heart-shaped face. Her big blue eyes were lined with the barest hint of makeup, and her lips were a bright hot pink that instantly made me hard, because I suddenly associated bright pink with her underwear and ripping them off. Her white off-the-shoulder dress was so pretty I was afraid to touch it—to touch her.

"Hi." Her smile was shy.

I wanted to pull her into my arms and kiss her.

I wanted to tell her how beautiful she looked.

I wanted to ask her if she regretted the cabin.

"Keaton! Beautiful! Turn around. Who are you wearing?" Media shouted louder for her than they had for any of us, and I knew if I kissed her, touched her, did anything that would show that I'd seen her naked—that I wanted to see more—they would have a field day.

I reached for her instinctively and didn't miss the flinch on her face as she turned away.

Rejection slammed into me. It's not like I was going to maul her on the stairs. I was going to kiss her cheek and tell her she was beautiful. Instead, one slight move from her was all it took to ruin the entire night and remind me yet again what people thought of me. What she thought of me.

Rachel Van Dyken

Julian Tennyson, bad boy of the finance world, did not touch pure Hollywood royalty. Lesson fucking learned.

Keaton looked over her shoulder and waved while people screamed louder and then faced me again. "Happy birthday, by the way."

"Thank you." I was just about to offer her my arm when a man I didn't recognize walked up and grabbed her hand.

Seriously? I can't even kiss her cheek and this bastard gets to touch her? My eyes narrowed into tiny slits. I'd never been the kind of guy that resorted to violence to get what I wanted—I had too much money to need to.

But right then? I was ready to shove him down the stairs.

"Sorry I'm late, K. It was madness getting in here." He bent over and kissed her cheek then faced me with a wide, way-too-attractive-to-be-touching-her smile. "Hey! Happy birthday. You Julian or Bridge?"

I couldn't keep my lips from pressing into an irritated line as I shook his hand and looked between them. "Julian."

Defeat didn't even cover it.

"Well, thanks for inviting us, this is great publicity for Keaton's new charity, and I think it will—"

She elbowed him. "Don't mind Rob. His sole focus is business."

"Like someone else we all know." Izzy laughed softly. "So Rob . . ." Bless her, she glided right in, took his hand, and led him into the building. "What is it you do?"

Bridge followed, leaving me and Keaton. I held out my hand and she hesitated, briefly looking uncomfortable as people shouted questions about us being together.

And that was when it hit me.

She didn't want people to assume anything about us.

I wasn't a man she would be proud to have on her arm, was I?

I'd never been a dirty secret until that moment.

And I'd never felt so low in my entire life, not even when I woke up from that coma. Not when I saw my brother and my fiancée kiss.

142

Nothing compared to the pain I had in my chest when Keaton looked at the media before tentatively grabbing my hand like she was afraid touching my skin would transfer all my sins to her.

Anger swiftly replaced the hurt as I gripped her soft fingers, careful not to hurt the tender skin that was still healing. "Had I known you'd be embarrassed to hold my hand, I would have let my brother do the honors. After all, we have the same taste—"

I barely had the words out when I suddenly tripped.

Keaton smiled through her clenched teeth. "Don't insult me, it's beneath you."

"Did you just trip me?"

"Yup." She popped the *p* as we walked into the Great Hall. Dark purple lighting made it hard to see. It didn't help that the centerpiece of each table had a water feature at least three feet tall. Izzy had clearly spent a fortune, and I was still so mad I could barely register how nice of a gesture it was.

I wanted to leave and lick my wounds in private. "So, Rob seems nice."

Keaton was still holding onto my hand. "He's a good man."

"Great," I muttered.

"Something wrong?"

"No," I said in a clipped voice, reaching for a glass of champagne and wishing I was already drunk off my ass. "Everything's great."

"Liar." She reached for a glass and faced me. "Been busy?"

"Small talk?" I snorted out a laugh. "Really?"

Her face paled a bit, and I know I didn't imagine the guilt that replaced it as she looked everywhere but my eyes.

I shook my head and leaned in. "Don't, not with me. I'm not one of your fans, Keaton, I'm not someone you need to be fake with. I get it, you don't want people to assume you're with me, fine. I imagine my father's smear campaign did a stellar job of scaring you away from me.

I don't even want to think what you'd see if you did a Google search on me, but could you at least for my sake, on my birthday, do one thing?"

Her eyes locked onto mine. "I didn't do a Google search."

I sighed. "One thing, I want one thing for my birthday."

"What?"

"I want you to pretend that I'm good enough to kiss you, good enough to touch you, I want you to lie to me and tell me it's just the beginning, that you don't care about my reputation, that you'd go home with me in a heartbeat because you can't imagine being anywhere else. Can you do that?" I checked my watch. "For one hour. I just want one hour where—" I stopped myself.

"Where what?"

"Would you believe me if I told you that you're the eye of my storm? The calmest part of my life when everything around me is chaos?" I set down my champagne at a table as more people filtered into the party.

Keaton reached for my hand again and held it tight. "Rob's my publicist."

"I didn't ask."

"You didn't have to." She dragged me toward the dance floor and then placed both hands on my shoulders. "I could see the jealousy in your eyes and the smoke coming out of your ears."

I glared. "I wasn't jealous."

"Oh?"

"I was just silently communicating with the universe and letting it know that if Rob were to fall down the stairs and break his leg I wouldn't be mad."

She threw her head back, laughing, and blurted, "I missed you."

I went completely still. It was on the tip of my tongue to say *"I missed you too,"* but her rejection was still too raw. And this insane feeling in my chest kept telling me there was more, that it wasn't just an accident, it wasn't a one-night stand.

She sobered and looked down. "My hands feel better."

I twirled her and pulled her against my aching chest. I'd been born to pretend like nothing affected me. I'd always had the upper hand—until Keaton. "Good."

"The doctor said that you did a good job treating them."

I couldn't look away from her blue eyes. I wanted to kiss her so bad that it was physically painful to be that close to her.

She licked her bottom lip, tempting the hell out of me.

I groaned and looked away. My body was reacting violently to the closeness. I was thankful it was dark because I was ready to pound nails into the nearest statue and have a mental breakdown in the process.

I was so focused on holding it together that when someone bumped into Keaton, forcing her to press her entire body against mine, I didn't think, I just grabbed her and held on tight.

Her eyes widened a fraction of an inch. She swallowed slowly, like she was trying to process the fact that I was so incredibly aroused it was embarrassing.

For both of us.

Instead of jerking away, though, she leaned up on her tiptoes and whispered in my ear, "It's not *my* birthday, and yet I still get a present?"

I let out a low growl and gritted my teeth. "Don't tease me."

She shimmied against me. "Oh, and *I'm* the tease?"

My dick was seconds from disowning me for just standing there. I moved away from her and cleared my throat. "Enjoy the party."

"Wait, what?" Keaton grabbed my arm. "Where are you going?"

"Well, right now I feel like I'm going insane, so I'm going to go get enough alcohol to make my dick limp, and then I'm going to ram my face into the closest door in an effort to crack the lock so I can leave."

She frowned. "But it's your birthday, this is your party, I thought—"

"Yeah, well, I thought too," I interrupted, anger surging all over again. "I changed my mind, I don't want a present, I don't want any-thing, and I can't pretend. I'm not that talented. I've lost every single ounce of fake enthusiasm and laughter I used to possess, and now this is all I have." I threw my hands up and shook my head. "This raw primal need to rip your dress in half with my teeth, but not just that, because that would be easy, sex is easy. I want more, and that's the problem, Keaton. I want more of you. I have settled for enough my entire life, I want more than good enough. I want all of it, and the problem is you don't have that to give me, and even if you did"—I scowled—"I highly doubt I'm the sort of man you would waste it on. So yes, I'm going to leave my own party. Yes, I'm going to walk away, because one of us has to, and I'm pretty sure if you left first it would break me."

I'd said too much.

She was driving me insane, though, and it hurt. For the first time in a long time, I felt something real, something good, something I hadn't had with Izzy and couldn't explain.

Something I couldn't have.

Funny how you can have millions of dollars, the best clothes, cars, and still feel fucking empty.

I turned around and made my way toward the bar for more alcohol and mentally berated myself for being so honest with her.

I genuinely liked her.

And she seemed embarrassed to be next to me.

Karma was such an evil bitch.

I deserved it—probably.

Didn't mean I had to like it.

I held up two fingers. "Two shots, bourbon."

"Make that three," came a familiar voice.

I had no fake smiles left so I turned and glared. "Dad, nice to see you."

"Sheathe your sword, son." He grabbed his shot and held it up. "Saw you dancing with Keaton Westbrook."

"More like arguing," I grumbled. "But good to know you're not going blind. If you'll excuse me—"

"Your brother's poor manners are rubbing off on you."

I snorted out a laugh. "No, actually I'm just all out of fucks." I threw both shots back. "Enjoy the party."

I sidestepped him and made a beeline toward the back of the hall. At the Met Gala last year I remembered people sneaking off in that direction. If I couldn't find an exit, maybe at least I'd find some peace.

I was almost home free when someone grabbed my arm and turned me around.

"You don't abandon a lady on the dance floor." Keaton crossed her arms and then put them on her hips. "And you don't just confess feelings like that and stomp off like a petulant child."

"Are you scolding me for having a heart?" I leaned in and cornered her against the wall.

She put her hand on my chest. "You don't understand. In public I can't . . . it's different, we aren't at the cabin anymore, Julian."

"I wonder if that's how you would pen *our* story. Julian Tennyson, dirty little private secret . . ."

A sharp crack split the air as she slapped me across the cheek. It stung like hell. I hung my head while she glared at me, chest rising and falling as if she couldn't get enough air.

"You should go." I didn't want her to go. I wanted to pull her against me again. I wanted her to pick me despite the fact that it was all wrong.

"You're a jackass," she said through clenched teeth.

"I never pretended to be anything but," I said quietly while her eyes darted toward my mouth. "I never hid that from you."

"You're right," she whispered, her eyes wide, searching mine.

We were standing so close that I could smell the perfume on her neck and taste the champagne she'd just drank.

Keaton swayed toward me and then slid her hands up my chest. Our foreheads touched. "You're the worst possible person for me."

"Are you *trying* to ruin my birthday?" I moved my head to the side, inhaling the perfume in her neck, ready to lick my way down the delicate column and beg for seconds, thirds, fourths. My lips pressed against her skin, and then I gave her a soft bite. Goose bumps erupted.

"Damn you, Julian Tennyson" was all she said before jerking my head down for a punishing kiss.

I opened my mouth, took her in, all of her, and shoved her back against the wall, my hands cupping her breasts through her tight dress. I'd never been so thankful for a slitted dress in my life as she wrapped a leg around me and rubbed herself up and down.

Anyone could walk by.

Fuck. Them. All.

Because when Keaton broke off the kiss, she whispered, "I missed you more than I'll ever admit to myself."

I kissed her again and whispered against her lips, "I stalked your Instagram."

She smiled against my mouth. "I stalked yours."

"Come home with me." I tugged her bottom lip and changed the angle of my assault as I drank from her. "Please."

"Yes."

"Now."

"Right now?"

"Right the hell now," I growled, pulling away and grabbing her hand and then sadly dropping it as I walked ahead of her back into the Great Hall and out the front door with her trailing behind me.

I wanted her.

That was all that mattered.

It didn't matter that she hesitated to claim me in public.

I would have her in private.

All of her.

And it would be enough.

Fucking worst word in the English language.

Enough.

My heart reminded me it wouldn't be.

But I ignored it as I jumped into one of the many town cars and waited for her to slide in next to me.

And my heart broke a little bit—that when she followed me, she was covering her face.

Enough.

It would be enough.

I, however, wouldn't be.

Chapter Twenty-Five

It was a bad idea.

A few paparazzi saw us leave.

I knew it could end badly, just like I knew I couldn't stop following him even if I wanted to.

It was soon.

We were both raw shadows of ourselves.

And yet I kept planting one foot after another. Maybe it was the fact that he made me feel good; he numbed the pain. It wasn't fair. Then again, I knew firsthand that life rarely was.

We didn't touch.

The media could speculate all they wanted.

Speculation, however, could ruin anyone.

And I needed to not fail at this one thing—for Noah, for his memory. I wrung my hands in my lap as the car turned around the corner.

Next to me, Julian was silent.

No. This really wouldn't end well for us, would it?

We were polar opposites. The media painted me like a saint. And Julian Tennyson? Hell's number-one sinner.

I wasn't stupid enough to believe it was just mind-blowing sex.

It wasn't.

Not with Julian.

It felt raw, aggressive, violent in the way it crashed over me every time he touched me.

But no matter how many times I warned myself in my own head, my mouth still said yes, while my body begged for more.

The bright lights of the city only added to the effect as we went in the opposite direction of where I lived—to Julian's.

His building was brand new.

I focused on the modern colors, the browns and blues, the silver handles of the door as the doorman pulled them open, the light fragrance of vanilla and new construction.

The elevator and the dozens upon dozens of floors that would light up if we hit every button.

And still Julian hadn't touched me.

He hadn't said a word.

We stood side by side, awkwardly riding that car to the very top.

I exhaled when the doors opened to the penthouse floor.

Julian got off the elevator.

I followed him.

And with each second, my awareness of him skyrocketed to a painful degree, even the way he slid the key into the lock had me licking my lips in anticipation. And it wasn't just physical.

It was the fact that we would be alone again.

Just us.

Blanketed in darkness.

And for the first time since coming back from the cabin, I looked forward to the absence of light—because Julian was with me.

The thought was terrifying.

I barely knew him and already he was my real live version of Xanax.

The door opened.

And I followed him in.

I did that.

I made the choice.

The apartment was blanketed in darkness except for the ambient light from the nighttime city sky filtering through floor-to-ceiling windows. Beyond them was a gorgeous rooftop patio that opened up to a fire pit, a small plunge pool, and green vegetation, all overlooking the city like its own private oasis.

I loved it immediately.

"I love that." I broke the silence and stared out at the patio. "I would probably spend most of my time there."

"Hmm . . ." He stood right next to me and stared straight ahead. "I can't say I've even been outside yet."

I scoffed. "Why?"

"My mom." His voice cracked. "It was her favorite part about this apartment. I bought it because of her. She said it would be good for me, a stress reliever. I had a special bedroom made just for her. It had its own entrance, almost like a mother-in-law suite attached to the apartment." He cleared his throat, his sigh was heavy. "She never got to use it."

I reached for his hand and squeezed.

He squeezed it back then slowly turned me toward him, still clutching my right hand in his. "I lied."

My stomach dropped. "What do you mean you lied?"

"At the cabin." His eyes locked onto mine. "The first day we wrote a chapter of your book, I went outside and I had one bar. I could have called. I didn't want to call."

I exhaled slowly. "Why not?"

"I liked the calm," he admitted. "And maybe hearing about you and Noah gave me hope that the world isn't such a horrible, unfeeling place."

"It just feels that way sometimes," I offered sadly, lifting my free hand to his cheek. His eyes closed, his dark lashes fanning against perfect cheekbones.

We stayed like that a few minutes.

It wasn't uncomfortable.

Almost like we both knew we needed silence in between stretches of heavy conversation so we could process.

"We can't . . ." I didn't want to have this conversation but it needed to be had. "I like you, Julian, I do, but we can't . . ."

He squeezed his eyes shut. "Story of my life . . . wanting what I can't have, only after realizing I never had it in the first place."

My stomach sank. "That's not fair."

"Life isn't fair." He left me then, walked over to the sliding glass door, and opened it, letting in the noises from the city.

He didn't look back to see if I was following.

Slowly he shrugged out of his jacket, followed by his shirt as he pulled it over his muscled chest. Next came his pants, socks, shoes, and then he was getting into the pool.

I watched in fascination as he swam back and forth, smooth, easy strokes. I couldn't stop watching.

I was about to turn on my heel and leave him in peace when I remembered the reason for seeing him to begin with, his birthday.

He was alone on his birthday.

I couldn't even process that.

He was alone, and all he'd wanted was me, was to pretend that it was different, that we could be together.

The worst part was, he thought that I wasn't proud to be on his arm, proud to be seen. What he didn't know was that my reputation was built on shaky social media ground. People had adored Noah.

They would crucify Julian.

I felt protective of him.

Protective of this strange thing between us.

Being seen with him could jeopardize the only thing I'd promised Noah I would do. But not just that; Julian's life was already hell. If we started openly dating, it would be unbearable for him.

And nobody wanted to grieve in the public eye, least of all people who knew how unforgiving the media could be.

Keyboard warriors, in my opinion, were pieces of shit who needed to get a life and stop trying to direct ours.

I eyed the expensive stove and fridge in his fancy kitchen that looked like it could house a small family and made a decision.

I dropped my clutch on the white granite countertop, went to the fridge, opened it, and was successfully matched with a bottle of champagne.

I grabbed two flutes after rummaging around his wet bar and then joined him outside.

He was still doing laps.

The fresh breeze was cold enough to make my teeth chatter; the pool must be heated.

I walked over to the edge, hiked up my dress past my knees, and sat on the concrete while he kept swimming. He must have seen me because he immediately stopped and swam over. "Weren't you leaving?"

"It's your birthday," I whispered.

His smile was sad. "It's just another day, Keaton."

"No," I argued. "It's the day you were brought into this world, and even though I didn't know your mom, I imagine that was the happiest day of her life."

Tears filled his eyes.

They filled mine.

He looked away like he didn't want to talk about it, so I made quick work of the champagne bottle, popping off the top and pouring us two glasses. I handed him his and lifted mine. "To living."

His chest rose and fell like he couldn't get enough air in. "To living."

"And to being the charming twin." I winked, earning a laugh from him.

He raised his glass. "To the sexy twin."

"It's good we're toasting to Bridge too," I teased.

"Oh, princess, you really shouldn't tease." He set down his champagne and reached for me.

"You wouldn't." I tried to get to my feet. "Julian Tennyson!"

His wet hands touched my hips as he stood to his full height in the pool. My breath came out in a rough exhale as he moved between my legs. "I would."

"I'll get wet."

His lips twitched. "Kinda the point, princess."

"You'll ruin my dress and my makeup," I pointed out as another chill wracked my body. It wasn't the cold, it was him, all him, and his naked chest and the way he was looking at me.

Like he'd seen me naked and wanted to see more.

I couldn't catch my breath.

My body responded when I told it not to, when I very calmly explained to my pounding heart that we were sad, that we couldn't move on, not yet, not with him.

Anyone but him.

But the heart, stupid muscle that it tends to be, just pounded harder as he leaned in and pressed a kiss to the corner of my mouth and whispered, "Get wet with me."

I sighed as he very slowly pulled me into the warm pool and swam us backward to press me against the wall closest to the edge. The wall was completely see-through, the city looked so small beneath us. A rush of excitement washed over me as he wrapped his arms around my middle and whispered in my ear, "She was right."

I nodded. "It is beautiful."

"Mmm." His rock-hard body wasn't touching me, not yet, but I could feel the heat from it against the wet dress plastered on my skin.

I squeezed my eyes shut. "Maybe it's the champagne."

"What?"

"This." I didn't feel the need to explain to him what I was talking about. "I couldn't write without you, you know."

"Are you saying you need me?"

"Don't get ahead of yourself."

"I'll help . . ."

My heart wouldn't shut up as it hammered in my chest. "I thought I was supposed to give you a gift on your birthday, not the other way around."

"But you did."

I frowned and turned around in his arms as a chill wracked my body. "What are you saying?"

He lifted a massive shoulder, leaned in, and pressed a soft kiss to my mouth. "You stayed."

"I'm a lame gift."

"It's all I wanted," he said, quickly pressing his mouth to mine again, and then I was lost, completely absorbed in the way his mouth played with mine, toyed and teased, like we were the only two people in the world, like our pasts didn't matter.

It was everything I needed in that moment.

To forget that it mattered.

And kiss Julian so he understood that he did.

And always would.

He moved his hands to my hips, hiking my dress past them. This was happening.

Again.

And I was saying yes.

Again.

Because he felt good and it had been so long since something had felt good in my life, since something had felt right—that I clung to it—clung to him as hard as I possibly could and prayed there wouldn't be a catastrophic downfall for our end.

"Stop thinking." Julian pressed another kiss to my neck. "I've been doing enough thinking for a lifetime—" A hand reached for my thong and tugged it down. "Now wish me happy birthday."

I exhaled against his mouth and gave in to the moment. I dug my fingernails into his muscled back as he teased my entrance then went all in. There was no warning, and I didn't want one, I just wanted him, I wanted that moment where I felt whole.

And even though I knew it was all a dream based on grief and attraction, I let him in.

And I kept him there.

"Happy birthday," I whispered against his mouth. My head fell back with each powerful thrust. I had nothing to hold on to but him, it only pulled him closer, made me frantic for more as I tried hooking a leg around him, only to have him pull it up and angle deeper, causing me to see stars. "Right there, that's incredible, right—"

"Keaton." His voice was rough with strain like he'd been holding back for my benefit.

I opened my eyes and stared at him as the water lapped around our joined bodies, the lights reflecting off the pool, the two of us in our own secret world.

"I missed you too," I admitted. "A lot."

Our foreheads touched.

Another punishing kiss as my body slammed back against the tile wall, sending water to splash over the opposite end.

And as release came, fast and hard, he whispered against my mouth, "Good."

Chapter Twenty-Six

JULIAN

It was the best birthday gift anyone could have given me: Keaton Westbrook. But I wasn't stupid enough to think it meant anything beyond that night. Neither of us knew how to navigate any of it. I wanted to, I wanted to ask her if it was possible. She made it easy to talk, just like she made it easy to mourn.

I both loved and hated that about her.

She didn't sugarcoat anything and was silent when silence was needed for reflection. She was everything I hadn't thought I needed in a partner.

Basically, she was perfection.

We were both quiet afterward. I grabbed a towel for her and turned around while she pulled off the wet dress. Even though it didn't matter, I still wanted to show respect, and I knew if I looked I'd ask for more. And I was pretty sure that wasn't something she was willing to offer or even give.

I went in search of something for her to wear and came back to the living room to see her wrapped in nothing but the towel, her eyes looking everywhere but me.

"Let me guess." I sighed and held out a pair of black sweats and a white T-shirt. "You never do this?"

Her eyes met mine, narrowed, and then she grabbed the clothes from my hand and strutted past me only to let out an adorable little growl as she turned back on her heel and faced me. "I wasn't going to say that, and you know I don't, and it's not funny to throw it in my face. I am a mature female adult, and I can make my own sexual choices . . ." She licked her lips. "At midnight. With a man who probably gets his dry cleaning delivered on a daily basis and doesn't even own a washing machine."

I smiled so hard my face hurt. "I like the top-load best."

She scowled. "Do you even know how to separate clothes?"

"It's not hard. Do you need me to show you a little domestication, princess? Because if you need a tutor . . ."

She held up her hand. "Never mind. I'm going to go change, and then we're going to set boundaries for this."

"This," I repeated, as my heart picked up speed from a dead stop. "Us?"

Her shoulders stiffened. "Well, yes, but not like you mean. You said you'd help with the book, right? Well, this is me asking for help."

My smile fell.

She hadn't had sex with me so I would help her, right?

When had I ever even doubted or cared?

I'd never felt like a one-night stand more than in that moment, like she'd given me something she rarely gave anyone—and now needed me to do something that only I could do.

It sucked.

Made me want to lash out.

159

To make her feel bad.

To make her feel pain and rejection all at once.

But her expression was so innocent. Was I reading it wrong?

"Please?" She touched my arm. "I need you."

I was an idiot.

An idiot who was going to die alone with memories of the way her skin tasted on my mouth. "Okay."

She exhaled and then wrapped her arms around my neck, kissing my cheek. "Thank you."

I waited until she was down the hall to breathe.

A door closed. She'd found the bathroom, good.

And I stood there, just listening to the silence, if that was even possible, and wondering how the hell I was going to keep my hands off her so we didn't have sex again.

The first time was an accident brought on by a secluded cabin and too much grief.

This time was a pity fuck on my birthday.

Next time, if there was a next time, it wasn't happening unless she gave me everything, unless I knew going in that there wouldn't be a chance she could walk away.

Next time would be a battle.

And I would be sure to win that war.

I just had to help her.

And do something that I'd never been able to do in all of my years on this planet—make her fall in love with me.

And not fuck it up.

Make her fall in love with me.

And stay.

All I had to do was compete against a guy who was twice the man I'd ever be, one who's going to be memorialized in a book that will most likely be made into a movie.

Compared to him for the rest of my life.

Huh, at least that wasn't a new battle.

No, it was one I knew how to wage very well.

And this time, I was going to win.

"Do you have a driver on staff or—" Her voice echoed around the vast living room as she made her way over to me, not finishing her sentence but staring at me with narrowed eyes like she could read my mind. "You look creepy."

"I was thinking." I rolled my eyes. "Don't read into it, and yes, I actually do, but I have a better idea."

"I'm not spending the night."

I grinned. "I didn't hear myself asking you."

She jerked back.

Shit.

"Don't look so offended. You know you would have said no anyways." I licked my lips. "Right?"

She rocked back on her heels. "Right. Totally."

"Uh-huh." I reached for her hand. "So I've been on a forced vacation by the board of my own company. Seems like they're afraid I'm going to have a nervous breakdown, and before you ask, no, I'm not going to have a breakdown, they're just paranoid and think I need time, blah, blah, fuckity-blah—" I shrugged. "We need a space where we can work without being interrupted or seen, right?"

She nodded. "Social media can be . . . ruthless."

"Great. So we work here, order takeout, put in long hours—something I'm very used to doing—and get the book done. Then you go back to your life, and I go back to mine." I smiled, sealing the deal. "Easy."

Her eyes narrowed. "There's a catch here."

"No catch. I want to help you. I at least owe you that since we aren't going back to the cabin, though you should know it's yours for whenever you want to continue your vacation, or I'll just reimburse what you paid."

She looked skeptical.

Shit, was I selling her too hard?

"What would you possibly get out of helping me? I feel like I owe you something. I mean I was serious when I asked. I just didn't think you'd be bored enough to say yes."

"It's not boredom," I said smoothly.

"Then what is it?"

Lie.

Lie.

Lie.

But I couldn't. It was on the tip of my tongue, but I knew I couldn't do it, not to her face. "You. I get to spend time with you."

A tentative smile grew. "You realize you don't get sex every time you finish a chapter."

"Absolutely." I nodded seriously. "As long as you realize you don't get anything until you say the magic words."

"'Please'?"

"You'll figure it out when the time comes."

"You're confusing me."

"Good." I winked. "Now let me call the car. I expect you to be here at nine in the morning with donuts."

"Wait, why am I bringing the donuts?" she wondered out loud as I typed a text to my driver, who was probably downstairs waiting out of sheer habit.

"You're the one who needs help. Ergo you bring the donuts for me to consume, and I'll try to call it even."

She rolled her eyes and laughed. "Yeah, right, a businessman calling us even over donuts? Why don't I believe you?"

"Why, I don't have the faintest clue." I leaned close and pressed a kiss to her cheek. "Be safe."

Her eyes softened. "I always am."

I didn't want to let her go.

I wanted to convince her that she should stay, preferably in my bed. I wanted to ask her if I could hold her, and pathetically enough I was so desperate I would even just take her friendship over anything else.

She left.

The door shut with finality behind her.

And I was blanketed in the depths of my own loneliness and mistakes once again, stuck wondering if my mom was watching, if she had been instrumental in bringing this woman into my life, and wishing like hell she was there so she could give me some wisdom on how to keep her.

A grieving girl who worshipped Noah.

A grieving man who missed his mom.

The only thing we had in common was our grief and money.

Maybe that would be enough.

For now.

Maybe *for now* was all I needed.

I grabbed the rest of the champagne from outside and carried it into my bedroom. I drank from the bottle and winced, even though I was doing what I typically did every night. Because tonight was different, it was my birthday, so I tortured myself with memories by clicking to the saved video on my TV.

With tears in my eyes, I watched my mom sing "Happy Birthday" to me at the cabin on my tenth birthday.

"Happy birthday to you! And you!" She burst out laughing as Bridge and I fought over the cake, and then she held up two forks. "Before you dig in, I have to make my speech."

"Aw, Mom!" Bridge groaned. "We have the speech memorized!"

"Can't we just eat?" I said in a whiny voice that made me want to punch my ten-year-old self. "It's gonna melt!"

"It won't melt, it's not ice cream cake," Mom scolded. "Now listen, one day you're going to be old like me, one day you're going to have the world at your feet. The most important thing to remember is that the world needs good men in it. Not powerful men, good men, men who are passionate about what they do, who want to make the world a better place. Remember, who you are defines what you are. You may be a Tennyson . . ." She hesitated like she hated the name. "But you're half mine, and you were born for greatness like the world has never seen. Love hard. Serve others. And most of all . . ." She trailed off.

We both jumped into the air and shouted, "Make Mom proud!"

I flipped off the TV in disgust as tears streamed down my face.

"I haven't been . . ." I whispered to myself. "But I think my penance is about to start . . ."

Mom knew and still loved me.

She was gone and she'd never gotten to see my true potential, all she saw was a carbon copy of my father, and in the end, a man trying to find himself.

I hoped that the universe was on my side, and I hoped that she would somehow know that I made it right.

Starting with the girl whose rose I'd crushed.

Whose heart I'd just ignored was breaking because I was too focused on myself, on my own pain, my own anger.

I would start with her, and I would let her go if she asked me to. Because that was what a true man did.

He didn't force his feelings, choking it out of the other person until they had no choice but to relent. He let them make the choice and honored it.

And if her choice wasn't me . . .

Then at least I did one thing right.

I made Mom proud in her death the way I couldn't make her proud in her life.

Chapter Twenty-Seven

KEATON

I clutched the box of donuts like a lifeline and looked behind me like the paranoid celebrity I was. I hadn't posted any pictures from the party last night and didn't see any speculation on where I was or what I was doing.

Which meant for now I was safe.

Plus, couldn't I just be visiting a friend?

A very rich friend who lived in the penthouse apartment and kissed like he was born to make love to my mouth?

I cringed as the lovely doorman let me in and nodded his head. "Mr. Tennyson is expecting you." He smiled wide. "Go to the top floor, he left his door unlocked and is running a bit late from his morning workout."

Wow, very detailed, this doorman.

I grinned at him and then opened the box. "A donut for your services."

He beamed. "I knew I liked you."

"Ditto." I laughed as he bent over the box. His black-and-white uniform was pristine. He pulled off one white glove and then winked up at me with crinkles at the sides of his eyes; his hair had speckles of white in it. He just seemed like a really happy person and easy. I liked him.

Especially since the donut he picked was the one with all the sprinkles. "Thank you, Miss Westbrook."

I almost corrected him, asked him to use a different name, then realized it wouldn't really matter, would it? Again, nobody knew what was going on.

We were working on a book.

No sex allowed.

My thighs clenched.

Damn it, why did he have to be so aggressive? I wanted him to slam me against the wall and pull all my clothes off and—

"Are you okay, miss?"

"Huh? What? Sorry." I closed the box and gave him a weak smile. "I'll just head up?"

"You go ahead, and thank you for the morning treat!"

God, he was adorable. I would bring him donuts every morning if he got that excited.

I quickly got into the elevator. Amazing how much faster it went when Julian wasn't standing next to me with all his masculinity pulsing in my direction, promising more kisses and orgasms than I could count.

Focus.

Today was about the book.

It was about Noah.

I squeezed my eyes shut as I felt my body deflate completely. Whenever I thought about Noah, I wondered what he would say to me about Julian. Would he tell me I was making a mistake? Getting in over my head? Was I betraying his memory by hopping into bed with someone so unlike him? Not that Julian didn't have his strengths. There were a lot of things about him that I loved.

And a lot of things that were obvious red flags.

I sighed as the elevator doors opened, then made my way over to his door and let myself in.

It was quiet, still gorgeous in the daylight, maybe even more so, because with the windows and patio there was so much natural light it made everything look even bigger, more impressive.

The man had absolutely no pictures in his living room of family or friends, which I expected, so I wasn't sure why it made me sad. Maybe because it was the same man that was going to spend his birthday alone.

My stomach tensed.

Nerves. It was just nerves.

"Oh hey, you're here," Julian called from somewhere behind me. I jumped a foot, turned around, and almost choked on my own spit. "I'll just be another five minutes, make yourself at—" He eyed the box. "Tell me those are from Big O Donuts, and you may just see a grown man cry."

I was still gaping.

Towel.

He was in a towel.

Protruding muscles clung to his midsection, even his neck looked thick, the rest of him was just damn pleasing, more pleasing than a donut, than a million donuts—wait, what did he ask?

I looked down and then back up. "Big O Donuts, the best orgasm of your life without sex." I shook the box at him.

Julian all but sprinted to my side and flipped open the top. "One's missing, there's only eleven."

I scowled. "I'll have you know your doorman deserves a raise."

Julian grinned down at me. "Trust me, I tip him all the time. He wants for nothing except for maybe female companionship and a few free donuts in the morning."

"He liked the sprinkles," I admitted.

"So you're saying you gave away my favorite donut?"

I stared at him, one eyebrow raised. "How was I supposed to know it was your favorite?"

"Easy." He swiped some maple frosting across his finger and then sucked it right in front of me, my mouth went dry. "The sweeter the better."

"R-right." I licked my lips, imagining the frosting there and then his mouth. "I hope you're not going to poke every donut with your dirty fingers."

"Dirty?" He dipped his finger in the donut again and then winked. "Just showered. If anything . . ." He eyed me up and down. "Let me get dressed and then we can get started."

"Yeah, dressing is good," I said like a complete idiot.

He just looked at me like he was trying to figure out whether I was day drinking, fantastic.

"I'll take this with me." He picked up the maple bar and left me alone in the kitchen, still holding the box and wondering why it felt so hot in his apartment and how I was going to survive every day in his presence.

And then I thought about the computer in my bag.

And the name on the flashing cursor.

Noah.

Usually when I thought of his name, guilt slammed into me; either that or utter desolation and sadness. Except in that moment, with donuts in my hands, in Julian Tennyson's apartment, all I could conjure up was one fleeting thought. That I would have liked them to meet.

Which made no sense at all since Julian was convinced that Noah would have hated him, but would he have?

Did it matter?

"Are you going to hold that box all day?" Julian came walking back into the room, dressed in something so casual I almost dropped the box.

"Are you wearing sweats?" I asked in a shocked voice.

He looked down at a pair of Under Armour pants and a vintage T-shirt, then gave me a funny look. "Are you gonna make it?"

"What? Me?" I quickly put the box down on the counter and took a deep breath. "I don't think I've ever seen you in anything so normal . . ."

"Well, strap in." He grinned. "I'm not going to wear a suit to sit on my own couch. Plus, I figure if we're going to hit your deadline we need to put in some hellish long days. I'm not doing that with a tie wrapped around my neck."

"Good point." I drew in a shaky breath and reached for my computer bag.

I didn't realize I was shaking until Julian's hand was on mine, and then he was squeezing it and turning me around to face him. "You're jumpy, what's wrong?"

He saw too much.

I knew it the day I met him.

He assessed.

He looked into a person.

He measured said person.

He decided if that person was worth his time.

And I was.

Worth his very valuable time.

"I don't know what's wrong," I lied. "It's probably low blood sugar. I need one of these." I snatched a donut. "And I'm stressed about this book. I just—I need to finish it and put it behind me."

"Understandable." His eyes searched mine. "Why don't you chew and talk, and I'll type out what you want me to type out?"

"Yeah, that's good." I took another bite and flinched when he leaned over and brushed his thumb across my lower lip. "Crumb?"

"No, I just needed an excuse to touch your mouth." He grinned. "Yeah, there was a crumb."

I liked the first answer better.

It was going to be a long day.

Chapter Twenty-Eight

"What do you mean the treatment isn't working?" I asked the doctor for the third time, even though I understood the words he was saying to me. I couldn't seem to let them sink into my consciousness.

Not working.

By themselves, they're boring words, hardly worth noticing.

But when a doctor says them to you.

About someone you love.

They suddenly have the power to strip every single ounce of energy and strength in your body and replace it with fear and disbelief.

Dr. Mark was in his midseventies and was one of the best oncologists in the tri-state area. If he said it wasn't working.

It wasn't freaking working.

Next to me, Noah didn't even tense. Already he was starting to lose his hair. The treatment was extremely aggressive. We were prepared for the worst, the worst being having to stay in the hospital longer than we originally planned. They needed him hooked up every six hours, so it just made sense to stay.

I made his bed my own.

We read a lot.

And binge-watched TV like it was our job.

Dr. Mark ran a hand through his gray hair and gave Noah a look I didn't recognize, one that had Noah squeezing my hand like I was the one that needed comfort.

"The hospital received a generous donation a few months ago. We were able to open up one of the old hospital wings and let family stay there. There's a kitchen near the old nurses' station, snacks, food, and each room has a bed in it that's better than the one Noah's in now. It might make things more comfortable while we decide what to do next."

I exhaled. "Actually, that would be great. I'm sure Noah's tired of this room."

"Preach," Noah joked with a rasp in his voice. "No offense, but this room sucks. I would do anything for a bigger TV and a bed that had pillows that weren't flat."

Dr. Mark grinned. "Yes, well, the donation was large enough that the donor even hired an interior designer. He felt new decor would help cheer up the patients, along with the family members staying here."

"Huh, remind me to tell him thank you," I teased, reaching for Noah's hand.

"He's here." Dr. Mark shrugged. "Somewhere, I think visiting his mother. I'll relay the message."

I barely heard what he said because Noah was looking at me like we were going to be okay. Like this was just another unplanned stumble before we hit the finish line and rang the bell cancer-free!

It was going to be fine.

His look told me so.

But I would look back on that moment, I would replay it over and over in my head, until I was sick with it because Noah wasn't squeezing my hand to tell me everything was going to be okay.

He was squeezing my hand so I knew . . . that he was okay with dying. Two weeks later, he drew his last breath.

But those two weeks were some of the best of my life, all because some rich person who didn't know us made the hospital into a home.

It gave us normalcy we didn't realize we needed.

It gave us the privacy we craved.

And that night, I fell asleep with a smile on my face while Noah held me, fully believing everything was going to be fine because we were in a normal bed.

I was wrong.

I stopped talking.

Julian stared at the computer screen, his face completely white.

"Sorry." My voice cracked. "I didn't mean to talk that long. It all just kind of . . . came out."

"It was perfect." He still wasn't looking at me.

"Julian?"

"I didn't know."

"What?"

"More than a year ago, the accounting firm I work with told me I had an excess of money I could donate or contribute . . . I chose the hospital because it would make me look good. I donated five million dollars because it would land me in the papers, because it was good business. Don't you see? I can't think about it without wondering how fucking selfish a person could be. I wanted praise for donating money, not even realizing that less than a year later I'd be in that same hospital fighting for my life, and unfairly winning while Noah had lost his fight. This right here tells me one thing, Keaton: life is fucking unfair." He slowly got up from his seat and walked into the kitchen.

"You can't think about it like that," I said softly as I followed him. "You know what's crazy?"

"What?" He didn't look at me.

I reached for his hand and then bypassed it and cupped his face between my palms. "I don't pray. Ever. I don't think it works. I think it's a fairy tale you believe in so life isn't so depressing—or at least I used to think that, but that morning I prayed, I prayed for more time with Noah, and then when they let us stay in the family wing, I closed my eyes and I smiled and I thanked God for the stranger with all the money—and prayed he'd know one day how much it meant to have a fluffy pillow and a down comforter, to go to sleep and know that Noah wouldn't wake up with a sore back in scratchy sheets—crazy how all that time, I was praying for the very man who would one day help me write our story."

Julian was silent, his eyes glossy.

I leaned up on my tiptoes and pressed a chaste kiss to his mouth. "In case it hasn't made it into your thick skull, thank you, because even if an act is intentionally selfish—that doesn't mean it can't turn into the most selfless thing you'll ever do."

Julian stared down at me. "How is it you can make me feel better when I don't deserve it?"

"You helped a lot of people."

He looked away from me. "And yet all I was focused on was helping myself, a happy accident, that's what that is."

I frowned. "You were at the hospital visiting your mom."

He stilled. "Caught that part of the story."

"I bet she was proud of you for doing that," I said quietly. "Regardless of your intentions, it was a good thing. Own the good thing, ignore the rest."

He looked at me then, his smile sad. "You deserved more than a fixed-up hospital room in your last days with Noah, you deserved everything."

Tears filled my eyes. "Good thing my book partner got it for me."

He started scowling again, which made my chest hurt more than I thought possible. I grabbed him by the face again and pressed a hungry kiss to his mouth.

I had no idea what I was doing.

Making him feel better?

Making myself feel better?

If I was being completely honest, it was this intrinsic need I had to make him smile, to make him understand his own worth. Julian didn't see himself the way the world saw him.

All he saw was selfishness.

Funny, because despite his playboy reputation, the world called him generous.

And he was.

Generous with everything, including his kisses as he slid his tongue into my mouth, his hands finding my hips and lifting me onto the counter.

He broke away and shook his head. "Sorry. I can't kiss you and not want more. We can get back to the book." His expression was shut off, distant.

I knew he still wanted me. I could tell.

It was hard to breathe with all the sexual tension filling up the space between our two bodies.

He paced in front of the computer like a caged lion, and I watched him like the antelope that was ready to volunteer as tribute to be his next meal.

I'd never in my life had such a violent reaction to a man—not even Noah.

Noah was all lingering kisses and laughter at first.

Julian was brooding, sexy, confused, and so damn lonely that my chest ached.

"Sorry." Julian turned around, his hands on his hips. "I'm ready for the next chapter."

He didn't want to talk about the elephant in the room.

The fact that we were writing a story he didn't even realize he was a part of.

I wondered in that moment if he understood that he wasn't the villain. No, Julian Tennyson had been my hero.

Chapter Twenty-Nine

JULIAN

She was staring at me like I was a saint when it was the last title anyone would give me, and I loved it, loved that she wanted to paint me like the hero for their love story.

And maybe that was the problem. It was another glaring reminder that just like her and Noah, this—whatever this was between us—would end, wouldn't it?

All good things did end.

I stretched my arms overhead and typed away for another four hours while she relayed story after story, some of them sad, some of them hilarious. I realized that she did better when I didn't interrupt her or ask if she was okay, so I let her go at her own pace and typed as fast as I could. At this rate, she would be finished with the book in no time.

Panic seized my lungs.

It was literally the only excuse we had to see each other.

And I knew I couldn't keep trying to seduce her, especially since the sex all seemed to have reasons around it: sadness, birthday gift, and favor. What would we do when we ran out of excuses?

We weren't just two people who found each other attractive; we both had so much baggage I wasn't sure I could even afford the fee.

My fingers ached a bit as she finished with one last story where Noah asked her to shave his head so he didn't look like a Chia Pet.

It made me laugh.

He was brave.

Stared death right in the eyes and said, "I'm not going down without a fight."

I would like to think that I fought during my coma, but I don't remember anything outside of the accident and simply waking up to my world changed in a way I was powerless to stop.

Because that's what love does. It makes choices regardless of how you feel and asks you to come along for the ride even if your heart is shattering in your chest.

"Julian?"

"Hmm?" I looked up after typing the last sentence and waited for her to smile or say thank you. Instead, she just stared at me with a pale face. "Are you okay?" Panic seized my chest—she didn't look okay. In fact, she looked ready to either pass out or hurl.

Keaton nodded her head slowly, then jumped to her feet and sprinted toward the bathroom at breakneck speed. Freaked out, I ran after her without thinking about the fact that I wasn't her boyfriend. I shouldn't be so concerned that my heart felt like it was in my throat. Yet I was petrified.

My mom puked a lot in the end.

A lot.

It was a trigger for me, made me think of the fact that the infection was stealing all of her nutrients and purging them from her already shaky system. And if Keaton was puking, that meant something was wrong, something was very wrong. I shoved my fear away and gave myself a few seconds, took a few deep breaths only to hear Keaton groan.

"Ughhh, donuts," she grumbled.

I knocked lightly, hating that I was visibly trembling, freaking the hell out over something that was probably just Keaton not feeling good.

"Don't come in!" she said in a weak voice.

Fuck that. I would break down the door if need be. If she was in there suffering, there was no way, puke or not, that I was standing on the other side doing nothing. I wasn't that guy anymore, and she had to know that a few words weren't going to keep me from making sure she was okay.

Ignoring her, I let myself in and grabbed a towel, wetting it and turning to her just as she flushed the toilet and looked up at me with mascara running down her cheeks. She was still beautiful even with black trailing down her porcelain skin.

"Not one word."

I got down on my haunches so we were at eye level, and very slowly ran the towel across her cheeks, getting the makeup off, and then behind her neck, lifting her hair. I tried like hell to manage the shaking. The last thing she needed to be was worried about me when she was the one on her hands and knees in my guest bathroom. "Do you need to puke again?"

She shook her head slowly, strands of blonde hair flipping sluggishly in a kind of delayed reaction. Then she gave me a pitiful look that told me everything I needed to know. She wasn't feeling great.

"Okay." I helped her to her feet. "Okay. I think we need to get something other than donuts in your system. I don't really have much food. We can go out—"

She paled further. I wasn't sure if it was the company or the idea of being in public and feeling like shit, maybe both.

"Why don't we order in?"

She exhaled. "You really don't have to, I mean I should probably head home and—"

"No," I interrupted her. "You know what's worse than being alone on your birthday?"

Her lips trembled a bit as she pressed them together. "What?"

I tucked her hair behind her head and kissed her forehead. "Being alone when you feel like shit."

She exhaled like she'd been holding her breath and then nodded. "That's true. I don't know if I told you, but I'm crashing at my parents' apartment until I figure out what I want to do. They're not here, so it's just this big, empty . . . lonely thing."

"I know big, empty, lonely things well," I teased. "Let me take care of you, friend to friend."

She relented. "That would be good. I haven't eaten much, and I think it's just . . . a lot, talking about Noah, sitting here . . ." She gulped and looked into my eyes. "With you, I mean it feels heavy, I don't know how I ever thought I could do this on my own."

She wasn't on her own, though.

She had me.

I gave her an easy smile and said, "Then as your typist and friend"—*hate that damn word*—"I say we call it quits for the day, put on a movie, eat, and just . . . relax. Hang out. Alright?"

"You're not busy?" she asked in a voice that basically said *Please don't be busy.*

And I loved it.

I loved that she wanted to stay.

Even if it gave me false hope that we could be anything other than what we already were.

Maybe if we didn't have this book between us.

Maybe if we didn't have this guy that would be immortalized forever.

Maybe if it wasn't less than a year after his death.

Maybe if we were both normal.

I ignored the way my thoughts tried to steal all the joy I had at being able to take care of her and said, "The only thing I have on my schedule for the next few days is you." Right along with, honestly, wondering what the hell I would do when I had to actually go back to work instead of eat donuts with Keaton and live off the crumbs of her kisses.

She offered me a watery smile and then gave me a side hug that did more than cement us in the friend zone. It freaking catapulted us there with a giant middle finger.

And I was too far gone to even really care, wasn't I?

I would take whatever I could get.

"Pizza sounds really good," she said, interrupting my thoughts.

"Then pizza it is." I kissed her forehead and left her in the bathroom and went in search of my phone. The old Julian would have said something snarky about eating pizza, only because I'd always been so particular about what I ate, even shaming Izzy, when she was still my fiancée, for eating chocolate.

Shit, I *had* been an asshole.

With Keaton, I would be pissed if she went on a diet. I wanted her to eat, because eating meant she was healthy, it meant she was okay.

It meant no more puking.

It meant a strong immune system.

Already I was feeling better that it was just something minor, like emotional stress over the situation.

Strange how almost dying puts everything into perspective . . . even eating a piece of damn pizza.

"Extra pepperoni!" She appeared back in the living room looking like she needed to sit down.

So I ordered the pizza and a double order of breadsticks, then promptly grabbed a blanket and tucked her in tight on the couch. "Relax and I'll get you something to drink. Rosé good?" I watched some light return to her eyes and immediately exhaled in relief.

"Hmm, chilled?"

"Is there any other way to rosé?" I joked.

"Ah, he's got dad jokes." She burst out laughing.

"Hey, I can be cheesy." I winked, enjoying the way her laugh filled my empty, lonely apartment.

She eyed me up and down; red stained her cheeks. "Yeah, there is absolutely nothing cheesy about you."

The compliment would sustain me for hours.

Chapter Thirty

KEATON

I should have gone home.

The only problem? I didn't want to.

Something about being in his apartment, locked away from the world, felt eerily like being at the cabin. It was just us.

Well, us and the laptop, which seemed to be the only tether or reason for us to even be in the same building.

The pizza sustained me in a way that only good carbs and cheese could, and I found myself relaxing more than I ever had in my entire life.

It wasn't the rosé.

For some reason it tasted funny, so I opted for water and ate three pieces of pizza and side-eyed the donuts.

"Saw that." Julian smirked at me. "I'm almost jealous of all the looks you keep shooting that box, you're about to incinerate the cardboard."

I slugged him in the shoulder with a laugh. "Chocolate sounds good!"

"Chocolate always sounds good." He gave me a look I couldn't decipher, then lazily stood and made his way over to the cardboard box.

There were plenty left, but I wanted the chocolate one. He picked it up and held it out to me. "Is this the one you want?"

I could taste the freaking thing on my tongue, the chocolate frosting, the soft dough. Big O Donuts were legendary, and I was about to make that one my bitch.

I bit down on my lower lip and nodded excitedly as the sound of *Riverdale* filled the living room.

I would never get tired of the way Julian stared at me, or the sparkle in his eyes when he was about to do something that would make me grab something sharp.

He held out the donut until it was about an inch from my face, until my mouth was watering with excitement, and the bastard jerked it back and shoved half of it into his mouth with a moan.

"JULIAN TENNYSON!"

"Sooo good!" His cheeks were puffed out with half the friggin' donut, and I just snapped. Clearly, I was feeling better if I was ready to jump on his back, which is exactly what I did.

"Give it to me!" I pounded his back with my fists while he made a run for it to the bathroom. "Give me the donut!"

He ran into the shower with me on his back and put his hand on the knob. "Don't make me turn the water on."

"Don't make me claw your eyes out!"

He burst out laughing. "Fine, fine, you can have the other half."

"OH! I want that half too." I smacked him harder. "Cough it up!"

"I'm not regurgitating donut!" He slowly twisted the knob. "You'll have to pry it from my—"

I crashed my mouth against his in a moment of pure insanity brought on by pizza, two sips of rosé, and emotional trauma.

At least that was what I told myself.

And he really did taste like chocolate donut, the best kind, with sugar on his lips and frosting on his tongue.

I could feast on that sort of taste, on this sort of man.

He kissed me back. All of the donut was obviously already out of his mouth, leaving only bits of sugar behind, so why was I still kissing him?

Because it was him.

Because he made me laugh.

Because he made me feel safe and alive.

I kissed Julian because I was falling way too quickly for a man who was totally wrong for me, and I kept kissing him because once I'd had a taste, I was completely lost.

Slowly, I slid down his side until I was facing him in the shower. He was still holding the donut high over our heads. Then eventually it made its way down until it was pressed against my mouth.

He leaned in and whispered, "Bite."

My breath hitched as I took a huge bite, chewed, and then smiled when he dipped his finger in the frosting and smudged it across my lower lip.

His teeth tugged the soft flesh, making me moan out loud, and then his tongue was sliding across and sucking as though my mouth was made of sugar and he had to get every last bit.

He gave me another bite and did the same thing with the frosting, and with each lick my body lost more and more control until I was shaking with the need for more, just more of him, more of us. Heat exploded between us when I ate the last bite, his hands flew to my hair as he jerked me against his hard body. And every single part of him was like colliding with muscle and masculine aggression.

We broke apart, chests heaving.

"Sorry," he said between breaths. "I think I'm addicted to you."

"Me or the donut?"

His eyes locked on mine. "The way you taste would haunt me for life, the way you feel is so right that I can't stop touching you—fuck the donuts, Keaton, I just like kissing you."

A chaos of emotions hit me all at once.

We were in his shower.

Eating donuts.

Making out.

I'd puked two hours before, but that didn't matter to him now.

And this man, this very clever, gorgeous man, was taking time out of his busy life to help me write a book about the only man I'd ever loved.

It was almost too impossible to believe.

And then I realized . . . that was why Julian was special.

Because when he wanted something, he went after it full force, with all his soul—and all his heart.

Which just meant I needed to be more careful.

Because when hearts are involved they usually end up bruised or broken, and I would rather die than break this man's heart.

I wondered if he realized he still had one, even after his mom's death. It was just hidden beneath a lot of pain and sadness that I knew so well.

Grief was a giant.

It was a monster.

It demanded to be heard.

One day his giant would come knocking.

And Julian would have no choice but to let his heart break.

I only hoped I would still be here to help him pick up the pieces and to, of course, give him donuts between kisses.

Chapter Thirty-One

JULIAN

Kissing her was going to be my downfall, wasn't it? I pressed another kiss to her cheek and then grabbed her hand. "Let's go finish watching another episode, yeah?"

She looked like she was going to say something.

Her eyes darted between my mouth and my eyes. I was almost afraid to let her speak, because I was so damn worried she would say something horrible like "I'm sorry" or "It was an accident."

It wasn't an accident.

And neither of us were sorry.

But it almost felt like we needed to say that because there was someone between us, and even though logically I knew she wasn't cheating and that this was okay, I also knew that the chasm separating us wasn't going to just magically fill anytime soon.

There were too many obstacles.

Huge ones.

I smiled and wrapped an arm around her, then whispered in her ear, "I'm not sorry."

It earned me a laugh.

And then she leaned up on her tiptoes and kissed my cheek. "I am."

I paused. "What?"

She darted past me and ran into the living room, then very adorably grabbed another donut, and shoved it in her mouth.

It was the last chocolate one.

Should have known.

My eyebrows shot up. "Feel better?"

She nodded, because she probably couldn't talk with all that donut in her mouth, and I think my heart did something funny in my chest, because I couldn't look away, and my smile hurt my face.

She grabbed a napkin and sat down on the couch, and I walked over to join her. I wanted to hold her hand.

But I didn't know the rules.

Because we existed outside of them, and as long as we were in isolation it didn't matter, did it?

I reached for her hand.

And she let me.

Hours later, I still had no idea what the hell we watched. I was too focused on our hands touching, on the easy way she laughed when something was funny, or the way her eyes widened when something shocked her on TV.

And finally, the way she leaned her head on my shoulder and fell asleep.

That actually might be my new favorite thing.

I was careful not to wake her as I picked up her feet and laid her out on the couch, tucking a black down throw around her body.

Like a creepy idiot, I smiled when she made a noise in her sleep and tucked her hands beneath her chin.

God, she was pretty.

So pretty, so innocent looking that the guilt tried to climb back up through my throat, tried to force me to say words like *"I don't deserve you,"* or *"You should go."* Instead, thankfully, she was asleep. I tamped down the guilt, even though the laptop seemed to have a laser beam connected to it as I walked by.

How did a person move on from a past love when that one was still very much alive in the present? Because he was, Noah existed in her heart still, he was there every day in the book she was writing. How did you win that battle?

I had no fucking clue.

I grabbed a glass of water and set it on the coffee table along with a few stale crackers—it was all I had, but if she woke up feeling sick, I wanted her to have something.

By the time I made it into my bedroom, it was two in the morning and I was wide awake.

I hadn't finished watching the home video I'd started, and part of me wanted to turn it on if only so my mom could meet the girl I was falling for, even though I knew it was stupid. But something about my mom's voice coming across the speakers and the knowledge that Keaton was in the next room did something to me. It made my chest hurt and my heart slam against my rib cage like it needed a quick escape plan.

Even though it hurt, I pressed play on the TV.

I watched ten minutes of smiles and laughter.

Ten minutes that I still remember as if it was yesterday.

A snowball fight.

My mom won. Then again, she always cheated and had premade snowballs when she challenged us to a fight so she would have enough ammo to destroy both me and my brother with a few good aims.

"Not this time!" I roared on the video, running straight for her.

A battle cry followed.

Along with four snowballs all at my face. Mom was scrappy like that.

I went down hard. Bridge charged after me.

And tripped over his feet, causing our mom to laugh so hard that tears streamed down her cheeks.

It was bittersweet.

Then again, mourning always was. You remember the good, and oddly enough, the bad seems to exist in a gray area where your brain refuses to visit—but even though you remember all the good times, you realize that your memory is a fucking imposter.

I was once told that when the brain conjures up memories, physically and mentally it's like reliving what happened.

I call bullshit.

Because I would do anything to conjure up this memory and feel the snow on my face while hearing my mom's laughter echo through the trees.

No, memories weren't reliable. I stood by my beliefs.

"Hey," a groggy voice sounded, causing me to nearly fall off my own bed.

Keaton had the blanket wrapped around her. She was standing in my doorway with sleepy eyes and a small smile.

I couldn't press pause fast enough.

She turned, just as the screen froze on my mom's smile.

Keaton gasped. "She's beautiful."

I wanted to kiss her for leaving out the past tense.

"Yeah," I agreed, taking in my mom's jet-black hair and blue eyes. "Absolutely stunning."

"Your apartment is too quiet." Keaton made her way around the bed and sat on the opposite side like I'd invited her into my room. I was too surprised to respond as she made herself comfortable. "You left crackers and water. I woke up feeling like the biggest jerk on the planet."

Not what I expected. "What? Why?"

"You were talking about being selfish, and here I am, crashing at your apartment, asking you to help me write a book about my dead boyfriend. And here you are, in your room, still alone."

It stung.

I looked away as my stomach dropped and a heaviness settled on my chest.

And then her hand was on my arm. "What I meant to say, and didn't get across because I'm still tired, is that you're more selfless than you realize. You don't have to help me. You could tell me to go screw myself, you haven't known me long."

I let out a sigh. "Maybe I have bad intentions. Maybe I just want to fuck you again."

"Don't!" she snapped. "Don't revert to the asshole in order to protect yourself. That's not you anymore—you know it, I know it."

Damn it, she was right.

I still couldn't meet her eyes. "I really like you, but it's not just that."

"What is it, then?" The room was too silent, the confession in my head too loud.

"I lived my entire life trying to make my dad proud and finally realized that I would never be enough for him. My mom, however, was proud when I colored inside the lines, she was proud when I lost a tooth, proud when I didn't spill my juice, proud when I came home and announced I had made the basketball team. She probably said she was proud of me a dozen times a day, hundreds of times a week." I licked my dry lips. "Why the hell did I spend my life wanting to hear that one word from my dad when I was always enough for my mom? I ask myself this all the time. Why was I so blind? It's like being told every day that you're enough but not believing it because it's from the wrong source, but she wasn't wrong . . . and now she's gone."

Keaton sank onto the bed beside me and slid her hand to my shoulder. "Her absence from this earth doesn't make her any less proud, Julian."

I squeezed my eyes shut. "I should have tried harder, in the end, to make things right with my brother, been more charitable, to do—"

"Stop." Keaton's voice was soft, and she gave my shoulder a gentle squeeze. "You can't live your life that way, even if you fixed all of those things, even if you were the perfect son and you did everything right up until the time she died—you'd still doubt yourself because that's what grief does to you. It tells you that if you just knew all the little reasons, if you just did this one thing, it wouldn't hurt so bad. But that's a lie, death hurts. The only thing that's true about death is that it hurts those it leaves behind. Hurt is hurt, Julian. Let yourself feel it."

"Do you let yourself feel it?" I countered, finally meeting her gaze. "Have you cried yet?"

Her exhale was rough. "I'm afraid if I start I won't stop."

"You would stop," I whispered.

"How do you know?"

"Because"—I kissed her temple—"I would hold you until you did."

Her eyes filled with tears. "How would that help you?"

"Helping you helps me—but I'd like to think that somewhere, my mom would nod her head and give me a small smile that said that's exactly the sort of man she tried to raise me to be. It would be an honor, you know . . . catching your tears."

I leaned over and swiped my thumbs under her eyes. "I won't tell."

And just like that, Keaton burst into tears, and I pulled her into my lap and held her like she deserved, swearing to the universe that I would fight for her, fight for whatever this was, until my dying breath.

Chapter Thirty-Two

KEATON

I woke up in Julian's arms. They were warm, solid, everything that I'd come to expect from him—stable. Weeks ago, I would have laughed had someone said I would be waking up in Julian Tennyson's bed.

And now? I couldn't imagine any better way to wake up.

I used to sleep next to Noah, but I was always so worried something would happen to him that I woke up every hour on the hour.

I frowned harder, remembering all those times I would call his nurse, ask him if he ate, make sure he washed his hands over and over again.

I was more nurse in the end than I was partner, and that was the truth that I was afraid to talk about in my book.

You watch romantic movies about people falling in love and saying that they'll be with each other until their dying breath and it sounds so wonderful, but they leave out the messy part.

The puking.

The pain.

They leave out the side effects of that forever love and tell you it's magical when it's nothing like that in reality. It's a lot of sleepless nights, medicine, machines buzzing, and false hope.

"Hey." Julian's sleep-filled voice was so delicious that I wanted to make it my ringtone, which was crazy. I burrowed under the covers and pressed my hand against his bare chest.

"Hi."

"Here." He handed me something cold. An ice pack? I slowly peeled back the covers and stared at him. "For your eyes."

"Are they swollen?" I asked.

His smile was warm, lazy, and sexy all at once. "No."

"Liar."

He laughed. "Breakfast should be here in the next hour. I got bacon . . ."

I took the ice pack, pressed it against my eyes, and winced. "Bacon!"

"Knew that would excite you." He chuckled. "So I know we have some writing to do today, but while you were lying there snoring—"

"I do *not* snore," I interrupted.

"Sure, okay, you woke me up out of a dead sleep three times because I thought that the building was crashing down around us—"

I threw the ice pack toward him. It fell between us. He just picked it up and pressed it gently to my face.

"As I was saying before I was rudely attacked . . ."

I made a face.

"My brother wanted to have dinner tonight. Because of the promise I made to my mom, we started going out for these Sunday dinners. Do you want to come?"

I did.

More than anything.

"Where's the dinner?" I asked, hoping it didn't give away the panic I felt at being in public with him. I wasn't ready yet. The world wouldn't understand. When did they ever understand anyway?

Julian's smile was tight as he looked away. "Don't worry about it, I know you had a rough day yesterday and aren't feeling well."

"Julian."

He started walking away.

"Julian!"

He stopped at the door, hanging his head, giving me his back.

"I'm sorry, Julian, it's just . . . it's too soon."

"Too soon for you?" he asked without turning around. "Or too soon for everyone else?"

I opened my mouth to say something.

I knew he was right.

It wasn't too soon for me.

No matter how many times I tried to say it was, no matter how much guilt I inflicted on myself.

I wanted Julian.

I couldn't explain it with words, I just knew the way I had known with Noah, but I didn't know how to keep my promise to the man in my past and also be with the man I saw for my future.

The doorbell rang.

Julian kept walking, and the smell of breakfast filled the large apartment. I needed to apologize. I also needed food. I pressed a hand to my growling stomach and then very slowly got out of Julian's comfortable bed and made my way into the kitchen only to see a few Barneys bags sitting on the counter along with the food. "What's this?"

Julian looked up, his smile wasn't as bright as before. I wanted it back, I wanted the look he gave me this morning, I wanted his strong arms wrapped around me telling me he'd hold me until my tears were all dried up.

"Those are shopping bags," the smart-ass said.

I glared.

"Saw that."

He didn't look up. "And I figured you'd feel better if you had some fresh clothes that didn't smell like the guy you refuse to leave the apartment with."

I flinched. It felt like he'd delivered a physical blow.

"I thought I knew your size well enough after . . ." He cleared his throat. "Don't worry, I used a personal shopper, didn't leave my name, and told them to deliver everything to Barry the doorman. If anything, they'll assume he has a thing for women's athleisure."

I peeked into the first bag and found a pair of cute leggings that were one of my expensive guilty pleasures he couldn't have known about, along with a loose Adidas hoodie that I would have picked out for myself, a pair of multicolored Gucci sneakers, BTS socks, which made me smile, and a comfy sports bra. The next bag actually held a garment bag. Frowning, I pulled it out. It was a dress.

Julian went completely still.

I unzipped the garment bag. The dress was black, would hit mid-shin, and had feathers wrapped around the middle like a belt that then dangled down the front of the dress. It was absolutely gorgeous. "This is . . . beautiful!"

He walked around the counter and took the dress out of my hands. "Well, you should be able to find someplace to wear it, right?"

I frowned. "The yoga pants I get, the dress I'm thankful for but a little confused about."

"We should eat."

"Julian—"

"It's not a big deal, money is just money, you know that."

"Yeah, but that isn't just a dress," I stated plainly, while the bacon made my mouth water.

Julian slid a takeout container toward me and zipped the dress back inside its bag. "I couldn't help it."

"What do you mean you couldn't help it?"

The corners of his mouth twitched like he was going to smile. "The personal shopper sent me a few links of things to look at because I wanted to make sure you'd like the color, and this dress popped up—probably because she was trying to get a bigger commission—and I instantly saw you in it, your hair piled on top of your head, or maybe just falling across your shoulders, and the more I'm talking the more stupid I probably sound, but you had to have it, and I had to buy it."

I smiled wide. "Julian, you just bought me a three-thousand-dollar dress because I had to have it. I think you may be the best"—I almost said *boyfriend*, where did that come from?—"the best friend I've ever had."

He sighed and rolled his eyes. "Don't read into it. I'm still a horrible person, remember?"

"A horrible person who has good taste in Prada." I winked. "Thank you, by the way, for last night."

He sobered. "It was a pleasure."

I gulped and stared at his mouth. "I don't know what to do."

"Well . . ." He handed me a plastic fork. "First you eat some eggs, then some bacon, go take a shower, put on your clothes, and we'll write some more of the book."

"About tonight—"

"Like I said, don't worry about it." His smile was tense. "I keep forgetting, which is stupid, because I'm not forgetful at all. I just want you with me."

His words pierced my heart.

I wondered if he realized that he was perfect.

That any girl would murder me to be in my position.

"Thank you for breakfast," I said softly.

He poured me some orange juice. "Welcome."

"You keep waking me up with your staring," Noah said to me a few nights before his eyes closed forever. "I can hear your heavy breathing."

I rolled my eyes. "I'm not heavy breathing all over you."

He started inhaling and exhaling like he was trying to pass out. "Oh sorry, I was just trying to give you an example."

I slugged him lightly in the shoulder. "How are you feeling?"

"Oh, you know, it's three a.m., my girlfriend's staring at me like she's going to kill me before the cancer can, my everything hurts, I'm thirsty, my hair, which was my best feature, by the way, is completely gone, and I'm thinking about shaving my brows in the morning, you?"

I gaped. "How can you be so calm?"

"Keaton." He grabbed my hand. "What other choice do I really have?"

"Um, you could yell at how unfair it is, scream, punch a pillow, and take a razor to the middle of your doctor's head. I don't know!"

He let out a low chuckle. "You're scary, you know that? Why would I take out my anger on the doc trying to save me?"

"Because he isn't." I gulped. "Saving you, that is."

"But he's trying," Noah pointed out. "And that's all that matters."

No, it wasn't. But I kept silent.

"Look, my attitude, whether happy or sad, doesn't affect my outcome. I could rage for days and it wouldn't heal the cancer, would it? Or I could choose to be happy and optimistic and spend the minutes I have making the world a better place. Complaining's like a drug. It only makes you feel better when you take the hit, but once the high's gone, you need more and more until all you are is a grumpy crab in search of treasure."

"Was that a Moana reference?"

"This is why we're friends!" He burst out laughing, but I gave him a funny look.

"We're more than friends, you psycho."

"About that, I think we should break up."

"Don't make me suffocate you with this pillow."

"And to think my first impression of you was 'Aw, how sweet does that sexy girl look, and damn . . . that ass,'" he joked.

I just shook my head. "You're out of control."

"If out of control is wrong, I don't wanna be right." He gave me a goofy grin. "Come on, Keaton, let's at least admit that things are worse than we thought six months ago when I swept you off your feet."

I rolled my eyes. "There was no sweeping, only begging."

"Tomay-to, tomah-to." He wiggled his eyebrows. "The odds of me sur-viving this are slim, and I was going to wait until morning, but Keaton Westbrook, I release you from your promise to make an honest man out of me."

I gaped. "First off, we never had that conversation. Second, I'm not leaving your side."

"I'm not asking you to leave. I'm just trying to help your heart a bit."

"So you're dumping me?"

"Exactly." He patted my hand. "Sometimes you're so dense!"

"Huh?"

"You should buy a cat, a really fluffy one that looks grumpy all the time. I would be stoked if you called him Noah. Seriously, it's my dying wish."

"Noah, seriously!" I couldn't help but laugh. "I don't even like cats!"

"You'd love Noah. He's a trouper, loves food, and sleeps most the day."

"Odd how you and this cat have so much in common."

Noah gave me a warm smile. "Look, I know you think I'm crazy, but you only have so much room in your heart. If I break it now, then if the worst happens, you won't be as sad. You'll be more like, 'That bastard better die, he broke me!' Anger is way easier than grief."

I sighed and cuddled against him. "Sorry, I'm here to stay, you can't get rid of me."

He sighed back. "You're like fungus."

"You're the one in love with me."

"True." He squeezed me as tight as he could.

We fell asleep in each other's arms.

The next day he took a turn the doctors weren't expecting.

And I wondered if he knew, if that's why he was awake, if he felt some-thing wrong in his body enough to want to have that conversation.

Because it was the last one we would ever have.

He had a small stroke and couldn't speak anymore.

I stayed by his side.

I bought beanies for his head, helped him brush his teeth and use the restroom. I read to him and told him jokes, and the silence was almost worse than the cancer, because all it left us with were longing looks, and moments when he was too tired to stay awake, where I'd stare at him and wonder if I was going to be more caretaker than girlfriend.

And knowing that I would do it.

If that's what it took.

I would do it.

The days were long then, they were filled with laughter between us, though his laugh never sounded the same.

And they were filled with hand-holding.

See, that's the thing that nobody ever found out about us. Noah asked me to write our story. In fact, he begged me, and after his stroke he wrote me a note since it was all he could do.

"Tell them our truth," *it read.*

Our truth is messy.

It was upsetting.

It was also not what people thought.

He asked me out, and yes, we went on several dates. I fell in love with him, he fell in love with me.

But we had rules.

No marriage—his rule; he said it wasn't fair.

No sex—my rule, because I was trying to make him wait until he was healthy. Wanted him to look forward to something. We loved each other in other ways, and we weren't exactly saints in those hospital rooms (sorry, docs!). But something I used as a carrot for him ended up being something he refused to relent on as he got sicker, not because he couldn't, but because he had this strange set of morals when it came to his life.

He didn't want to marry me because he said it would be taking away my first marriage if something happened to him. It was like stealing me from someone else.

And when we found out he was terminal, he said he didn't want me to torture myself with memories of how insane he was in bed and compare every poor guy to him, knowing they would never measure up.

It was a running joke.

One that got less and less funny as he got sicker.

So yes, he was my boyfriend.

Yes, we were in love.

No, we never slept together.

And yes, he dumped me before his stroke. In fact, everything Noah did was for me, for others. He lived selflessly, fearlessly, and I'll never forget the way he ran toward fear, the way others run from it.

Julian was quiet except for the soft tap of the keys. We'd been at it again for a few more hours, only this time he had more food delivered. As long as I ate, I didn't feel sick. I was going to take a long vacation once this book was done. Emotionally, it was wrecking me, and taking a physical toll on my body.

"You never slept together." Julian stared at his computer in disbelief. "I don't know if I want to shake him for being so stupid or thank him for saving those parts of you for me."

I sucked in a shocked breath. I couldn't deny the truth. I wondered how I would have felt had I given everything to Noah . . . and then slept with Julian. "You made fun of me when I said I don't normally do this. I don't." I smiled weakly.

"He was a good man, Noah," Julian said, emotion thickening his voice, and then he stood. "I need to get ready for dinner."

"Yeah, okay." I tucked my hair behind my ears. "I should probably head back to my apartment and shower, clean up and—"

Julian was in front of me in an instant, then his mouth was on mine, softly teasing, coaxing my lips apart before pulling away. "Grab an overnight bag."

"But—"

"Don't argue." He kissed me again. "Just until the book is done."

I smiled against his mouth. "Why does it feel like you're lying?"

He sighed then moved his mouth down my neck, his nose tickling my skin as he inhaled and whispered, "Because I'm going to keep coming up with excuses. I like my apartment better with you in it."

I liked my life better with him in it. "I do too."

"Good." He kissed the top of my forehead. "When you need a ride, just call down to Barry, and he'll have one waiting for you up front."

I nodded and watched him disappear into the bathroom.

I hated that he didn't try to persuade me to go with him, and at the same time I loved that he didn't try to manipulate my emotions. He wanted me to be ready to be with him. I wanted that too. I really did.

I just needed to figure out a way to do it without feeling like I failed Noah and all the people who had invested in our story. I wasn't falling, I was there, but my team had also been very upfront about the outrage generated by my last post. I mentioned moving on because I was trying to be inspiring, to offer hope, and instead my followers saw me as spitting on Noah's memory.

The last two posts I'd done had been about writing the book, and the comments ranged from "Glad you aren't moving on" to "You'll love him forever!" And it killed me inside to think about Julian reading those comments, believing them, or worse, coming under fire because he liked me and I liked him.

I didn't want to let down my followers.

But I also needed to live my life.

And I needed Julian in it.

Chapter Thirty-Three

JULIAN

"Hey, you made it!" Bridge walked around the table and slapped me on the back with one hand and then pulled me in for a hug I was ninety-nine percent sure was going to end up in multiple tabloids.

I understood Keaton's reservations.

Didn't mean it didn't burn or make me want to throw something.

"Yup." I hugged him back quickly and took a seat across from my ex-fiancée and my brother.

Had there ever been a more awkward third wheel?

Doubtful, highly doubtful.

I was ready to wave down the waiter and let him know to keep them coming when a drink appeared at my elbow.

"Bridge, know that I mean this with every fiber of my being—thank you for using twin sync, reading my mind, and ordering me alcohol." I threw back the glass of fine whiskey and was ready to hug him again when he and Izzy both gave me a funny look. "What?"

"Our waiter hasn't stopped by yet." Izzy grinned and then hid behind her menu.

"Izzy, if you set me up on a blind date, I'm going to officially lose my shit. I've been typing a love story that I'm not part of all day every day, falling for a woman who refuses to see me in public, and all I want is to get through dinner, preferably drunk so I can go home and repeat the torturous process."

Izzy's smile was so big I was almost nervous.

Bridge looked equally excited.

"What?" I huffed.

Someone tapped me on the shoulder.

I turned and nearly fell out of my chair as Keaton, in the black dress I'd purchased for her, pulled out a chair and sat down. "Not really a blind date if you already know the person, right, Julian?"

My smile was currently taking up my entire face. "You came."

"No thanks to you." She jabbed a finger in my direction. "I had to call Izzy to find out what restaurant I'd need to crash. Thankfully she called me back right away and offered her firstborn if only I'd show up and order you whiskey."

Bridge let out a snort while Izzy burst out laughing. And then Bridge elbowed Izzy. "You didn't really offer up our child?"

Izzy just patted his hand and rolled her eyes, reminding me why they were better for each other from the start, reminding me why we only ever had friendship and a tumultuous relationship where neither of us was ever fully satisfied but constantly trying to be something we weren't.

I could have sworn in that moment, Izzy knew the direction of my thoughts. She nodded her head slightly and lifted her water glass in silent acknowledgment of something I refused to decipher, but it felt a hell of a lot like waving a white flag and shouting, "Peace."

The waiter arrived before I could say anything, and then Keaton's hand was on my thigh, squeezing.

I didn't realize I'd been holding my breath until I exhaled and covered her hand, giving a return squeeze. She quickly let go, but it was enough for me to think that maybe this was a baby step in the right direction.

Both of us appearing in public meant nothing.

But to me it meant something.

It meant people would wonder.

It also meant that I would have to control myself when all I wanted to do was throw her onto the table and kiss her senseless for coming.

My eyes greedily scanned the menu, reading everything, under-standing nothing, because I was too focused on the woman sitting next to me, when someone cleared their throat.

It was a teenage girl. She was holding out her iPhone and staring at Keaton like Keaton was going to sprout ten heads. "Um, hi, you don't know me, and I know you guys are about ready to have dinner . . ." Her eyes fell to me in confusion then back to Keaton. "But could I get a selfie with you?"

Keaton beamed. "Of course!" She quickly got out of her seat while the girl jabbered on and on.

About Noah. "OMG! I followed your guys' love story and bawled my eyes out when he had his stroke and then to think you only had a few more days with him . . . I had to take a week off school. I'm still not over it." She sniffled. "Your love story is so beautiful!"

"Thank you." Keaton suddenly looked uncomfortable as she took a picture with the young girl and thanked her again.

"Oh, one more thing!" The girl smiled. "Do you plan to do any-thing for Noah's birthday this year? You know, like you did last year with the cake? It would be a really cool way to memorialize him, and I know your fans would love it."

Keaton looked ready to barf. "Um, maybe, it just depends. This is all still very difficult for me, and I'm writing his book right now."

"Ohhhh." The girl pressed her hands to her chest like she was going to cry. "That's so wonderful! So this must be a business meeting, I'm so sorry!"

Now I was uncomfortable as I looked from Bridge to Izzy, both of whom had frozen smiles on their faces like they were thinking, *Get this girl out of here before Julian pops a blood vessel in his forehead from smiling too forcefully.*

I was seconds away from that actually happening when the girl finally left and Keaton sat back down.

The entire table was silent, and then she said in a small voice, "Sometimes I wonder if they'll punish me for moving on."

Izzy spoke first. "It's not their call to make, Keaton."

"Kinda feels like it, though." She sighed and then frowned down at the menu. "Sorry," she said in a tight voice. "Sorry—I'll be right back." She shoved her chair away from the table and rushed toward the restrooms.

Shit.

She was getting sick again.

"Sorry, guys. She hasn't been feeling well." I pushed my chair back and followed after her as she vanished into the ladies' room. It was hell waiting outside the door, but she returned around six minutes later—yes, I timed it. "I need a toothbrush, gum, something . . ."

I smiled. "Fresh out of all of the above, but you could always swish whiskey around your mouth. Isn't that what alcohol does? Disinfect? Kill?"

She swiped under her eyes and laughed. "Good to know that we have the same beliefs about whiskey, though I don't think doctors use it on wounds anymore."

"Not true. They do use alcohol to disinfect," I pointed out, pulling her in for a small hug. "Are you okay?"

"Yeah, I think it's just this trigger now. Every time it feels like too much, my body just reacts, you know?"

"Yeah." I kissed the top of her head. "Let's go get some bread into you."

We rounded the corner, nearly bumping into the same girl from before. She eyed me up and down and then Keaton.

We both smiled at her but her eyes were narrowed into tiny slits like she was doing really hard math in her head.

I ignored the feeling in my stomach that said something was off and took Keaton back to our seats.

The rest of the dinner was nice, quiet, no interruptions, and once Keaton ate she was totally fine.

I was suddenly thankful I had taken the chance on the dress.

Thankful that I listened to my mom even after her death, even when it hurt, and thankful that the girl sitting next to me had actually joined us.

If only I could hold her hand and shout it to the world, that she was mine and I wasn't letting her go.

"So how is the book coming along?" Izzy asked once the dinner plates were cleared and dessert menus were distributed.

I let Keaton answer; it was her book. I was just helping her get it off her chest, sharing the emotional load, and learning about her every day, because his story was also hers.

"Well . . ." Keaton eyed the menu, then looked up. "I think we're almost done. Julian's been a typing machine. I don't know why but it's just easier talking out loud than typing it. Typing it feels so . . . final to me, and I get stuck, but talking about it just feels like a conversation, keeping the memory alive." She smiled over at me. "He's saved my entire book deal."

"Well, that's what Julian does." Bridge shrugged like it was normal. "He saves people."

"True," Izzy joined in. "When Bridge was struggling with his mom and they had absolutely no money, Julian built them a trust fund that would set them up for life. He wanted to make sure that Bridge wasn't cut out of something he was owed."

I didn't know what to say to that.

"Sounds like him," Keaton agreed as if I wasn't even at the table.

I shifted uncomfortably in my seat. "If you guys are trying to make me look good, it's working."

Bridge scowled. "You don't need help looking good. You have the better hair."

I laughed at that. "True."

Keaton and Izzy joined in until the entire table was laughing. And somehow, it wasn't awkward. The four of us together.

It felt a lot like coming home.

Like finding forever.

Finding my family again.

"Any dessert?" I nodded toward the menu in Keaton's hand.

She scrunched up her nose. "I think the chocolate mousse, wanna share?"

I gave her a knowing look. "If I say yes, you're going to grab your knife and hold it at my throat with one hand while you finish the entire thing, aren't you?"

She sucked in a breath like she was outraged, then said, "Yeah, probably."

"Sure, yeah, I'll share." I laughed, earning a curious look from my brother that basically said I was a goner when it came to Keaton, so I shot him a look that said *Shut the fuck up,* earning a wide smile and quick middle-finger flash that had me laughing more with him than I had in a long time.

They settled on the buttercream cake to share, though the minute it arrived, Izzy took both forks. Then again, she was pregnant, so Bridge didn't even argue.

Keaton dug in to hers with fervor. I enjoyed watching her eat it, and then she rolled her eyes and moaned. "Okay, I'm only sharing a bite so you understand this is why I would stab you in the throat, 'k?"

"Violent, isn't she?" Bridge said out loud.

"Threatened to kill me when we first met, so I'd say that's a yes," I joked and turned to Keaton. "Alright, let me have it."

"Oh, I'll let you have it so hard . . . ," she said more to herself and then looked up. "Sorry, I have a thing for chocolate."

"My kinda girl." Izzy reached across her table with her fork, they clanked them together in some sort of secret female ritual that basically conveyed not sharing. Ever. And laughed.

Then Keaton's fork was in front of my mouth. "Open."

I did as I was told, because Keaton and chocolate together were irresistible, and tasted the best chocolate mousse I'd ever had in my entire life. She pulled the fork back. I clamped down with my teeth and licked the rest of it, my hand grabbing her wrist while she laughed.

"How could you!" a voice shouted, causing Keaton to drop the fork.

My gaze darted around the room and settled on the girl holding her phone up at us, shaking with rage. "You promised to love him forever!"

Keaton opened her mouth. I shook my head at her and stood and went in search of security. Luckily, they were already on their way. It wasn't normal for any of us to be accosted during meals, but the restaurant always knew to be on high alert whenever a Tennyson was around—we had changed lives within the same breath of ruining them, and while my brother and I were trying to make the company better, we still had to deal with the aftereffects of our father and his ruthlessness.

"Miss, come with me." The guard stood in front of the girl as she looked around him at Keaton and shook her head angrily.

Keaton went completely still. Tears filled her eyes as the girl shrugged away from the security guard and started to cry. "I can't believe I used to look up to you! Were you even together? Was it just some giant publicity stunt to get Instagram likes? How could you even move on? Real love wouldn't let you! You're so fake!"

"That's it." The security guard physically grabbed her and moved her toward the exit, amidst all the hushed whispers around us.

I reached for Keaton's hands.

She held them in her lap.

And when I squeezed her thigh for comfort, she stiffened.

The rest of the evening was ruined.

And I had a sinking feeling that all of the progress we'd made together, dealing with our grief, the book, this thing between us, just took two giant leaps backward.

Chapter Thirty-Four

KEATON

I felt physically sick that night as I stared at the laptop. True to my word I came back to Julian's.

All that mattered was finishing the book.

Releasing it to the masses.

Moving on.

That and Julian.

I had no idea what to do. My followers meant the world to me, and for them to have the wrong idea—I didn't know if I should address it publicly or just lie low and let it play out.

Julian had gone to bed, saying he was tired, and I'm sure he was, tired of me not taking a leap, tired of me needing him and taking everything without giving him all of me.

I'd be tired too.

I stared at the laptop.

I hadn't touched the keyboard since the morning I'd found out about Julian's birthday party. It seemed like a lifetime ago.

I couldn't sleep.

And both Julian and I knew we only had less than two weeks to finish, though at the rate we were going, it would be done sooner rather than later, we were already at two hundred and fifty pages.

Already close to the end.

Part of me didn't even want Julian to type those words, though I knew they were necessary, and another part of me felt like I was the one who needed to do it.

I sat at the table and opened the laptop. It was on the last page Julian had typed out.

I frowned and scrolled through the last chapter.

In the margins, he had left comments like *That's my favorite part* and *Any man would fall in love with a smile like that.*

There weren't just a few comments but hundreds of them, about his own opinions, about how he didn't blame Noah, even some on how he was jealous of him.

I quickly shut the laptop, my body buzzing with awareness.

Julian had no idea, did he? That as he was writing the end of Noah's story—he was writing the beginning of ours.

Tears filled my eyes as I stood and made my way into the bedroom. Julian was lying there on his side, sleeping in all his masculine glory.

His skin looked tanned against the white silk sheets. He turned in his sleep, and the sheet fell past his abs down to his waist. A sudden craving for him whipped through me, and I licked my lips.

I couldn't compare them.

They were so different.

Where Noah was all jokes, Julian was more reserved.

Where Julian was more controlled and dominant, Noah was carefree.

I took care of Noah.

And Julian?

He took care of me.

This would be the moment where I should call my mom and ask for advice, but I knew what her answer would be.

Jump.

She was carefree just like Noah had been.

I bit my bottom lip as I watched Julian toss and turn. I wanted to fight his monsters, I wanted more.

"Noah," I whispered. "What do I do? How do I handle this?"

I squeezed my eyes shut as the sound of the TV got my attention. I hadn't even realized it was on.

Tears blurred my vision as I saw a commercial for adopting cats.

You've got to be kidding me.

Tears fell down my cheeks.

"Really, Noah?" I whispered through my tears.

"Hey." Julian's sleepy voice filled the room. "Are you okay?"

I turned to him, his concerned green eyes and his wavy hair, his perfect jawline, intense gaze, and caring attitude. He was a bossy ass who I was falling in love with despite my heart still belonging to someone who no longer had one that beat.

And it was time to jump.

"How do you feel about adopting a cat?" I crossed my arms.

Julian's eyes narrowed. "Are you drunk?"

"Come on, a tiny little kitten just roaming around—"

"Shitting in a box, in my apartment." He stared me down and then fell back against the bed. "I'm going to regret this."

"Yes!" I made a beeline for the bed and jumped on, then wrapped my arms around his neck and lay across his body.

"Is that the only reason you were hovering in the doorway watching me sleep?" He licked his lips.

"No." I grinned. "This is." I leaned back and peeled off my shirt.

His eyes drank me in. "This is better than a cat."

"We're still getting a cat." I kissed him hard on the mouth and pulled back.

"Sure, we'll go tomorrow." He kissed me back with a groan. "I'll get you ten fucking cats if you keep kissing me like that."

"They'll call us the crazy cat couple." I laughed.

"As long as we're a couple . . . ," he whispered in a serious voice, "let them."

I nodded, not trusting myself to say anything. He pulled back, his eyes searching mine.

I kissed him again and again.

"Keaton?"

"As long as we're a couple," I said against his mouth, "let them call us whatever they want."

His mouth came down hard, and I realized this was what I'd needed all along, to let go, to adopt a stupid cat, yes, but to let go and fall into Julian's arms, to give him an "us" to fight for.

In order for us to work, an "us" had to exist.

"Are you saying what I think you're saying?" Julian made quick work of the pajamas I'd brought, silk shorts came flying down my legs before I even had a chance to answer. His fingertips felt like velvet across my skin as I moaned his name.

"Mmmmm."

Julian kissed up my neck then pressed his lips against mine. "Tell me this means this is more than a writing relationship."

I laughed at that. "It's never been just a writing relationship, has it?"

He swallowed and then, "Never."

"I want to try. I don't know how, and we're going to piss people off, but—"

"All that matters is that I have you," he finished, his hands roaming down my body, making me forget my own name right along with all the reasons I had hesitated.

Why had I hesitated?

This was everything.

This felt so good it was painful.

His mouth moved down my chest as he flipped me onto my back and kissed every inch of skin like he wanted to make sure that anyone who came into contact with me knew who had been there. Julian Tennyson.

I didn't mind.

I dug my hands into his thick hair and held on as he pressed tiny kisses across my hips, bracing them with his strong hands, lifting my body up to his mouth like a feast he'd been waiting for, starving for, begging for.

His tongue was hot, lightning against my skin. A kiss on the tender flesh of my thigh, another closer to where I wanted him. With every pulse, every exhale, I felt him, needed more of him.

"Tell me you're mine, Keaton," Julian rasped, teasing me with a soft flick of his tongue followed by the palm of his hand. "I need to hear it."

I moaned. "I was yours the minute you asked me to build you a fire."

He chuckled darkly against my skin, and goose bumps erupted all over my body. Everything about him set me off. "And I was yours the minute you pulled a knife on me."

"Enough with the knife . . . ," I grumbled lazily as my mind tried to focus on words instead of what he was doing with his mouth, his hands, mouth, hands . . . I couldn't keep track. It was driving me crazy, so many nerve endings firing while time stood still for us.

This is how it should be.

Happy, not sad.

Hello, not goodbye.

That's what this was with Julian.

With Noah it would have been goodbye.

It broke my heart to admit . . . that he'd been right.

Because with Julian it was a fresh page, a new page. With Julian it said the beginning, with Noah it would have been tears because it was too close to the end.

I was close when Julian's mouth found mine again. He hovered over me, bracing his body, staring down at me with the sort of wonder people wait their entire lives to experience.

I kissed him.

Tasted him.

Moved my body in sync with his as he slowly moved inside me like he wanted to savor the moment between us—the moment we were each other's.

His green eyes locked on mine. "I never want to let you go."

"Who said you had to?"

Our foreheads touched. "You feel like something I've searched for my whole life without even realizing what it was—the treasure you know exists but can't fucking find." I gasped as he thrust deeper, rolling his hips, making me come off the bed like fireworks. "Being inside you is my heaven, Keaton."

"Mine too," I whispered with another groan as tiny spasms grew, like little bursts of sunlight exploding between us, the world could burn down and I would stay there forever, in his arms.

Our mouths fused as I clung to him, holding him close as he moved fluidly in me like we had all the time in the world, like we could make love forever in that bed.

I didn't realize I was crying until he swiped a tear from under my eye and kissed his fingertip like it was precious.

"I need you more than you'll ever know," I whispered.

His head touched mine, a graze of his lips as I felt him thrust deep, taking me with him down a road that would change us forever. "Good."

I let go.

Of not just my fear.

But of my first love.

Chapter Thirty-Five

JULIAN

I slept so hard that I woke up disoriented, until I felt Keaton's hot mouth on me, and then I just thanked God I was alive.

I gripped the sheets while she woke me up in the best physical way possible and nearly wept when she swirled her tongue.

"Shit." My hips bucked while my balls seized, ready to combust. I wanted to be inside her, I wanted her every way I could have her, but I couldn't find it in myself to even move. "Keaton, I'm going to—"

"Kinda busy . . ." Her head popped up.

And then I was done for.

Completely screwed and so damn happy I wanted to throw a parade for her and her mouth.

Keaton's head poked out from under the duvet. "Oh, hey, you're awake."

"I'm building a shrine to your mouth," I admitted in a sleep-filled voice.

She beamed. "Only if I can build one to your abs." She walked her fingers up my chest. I grabbed them and kissed the back of her hand then tucked her next to me.

Where she belonged.

"So . . ." I toyed with her fingers. "I figured we should work on the book for a bit, see how far we can get, and then order in."

"You don't have to order in. I mean we don't." Keaton looked up at me tentatively. "I decided last night, even though it makes me sick, to just keep living my life. They don't know my pain, my struggles. They don't know what I feel. If it gets really bad I'll address it, if not . . ." Her voice trailed off. I could tell it wasn't a flippant thing.

"I'm okay with lying low," I said seriously. "And you haven't been feeling good anyway."

"True." Her fingertips trailed my jaw. "How about we just wait and see?"

"I'm okay with that." My hand slid down to her ass and cupped her. "But I think I may need a few more minutes to wake up."

She rolled her eyes.

And then I gripped her by the ass and turned her to her stomach, moving my body over her. "Just a few minutes."

"Of suffocation?" she teased.

I bit her ear and tugged. "Pleasure."

"Yes . . ." It was breathless, needy, it was all for me.

In the last days, there was a lot of silence. It's not what you see on TV, where everything looks clean, like you're playing this waiting game until something works and kills the cancer. It's constant pain, constant wondering, questioning. It's not pretty. Death is the end of something that shouldn't die in the first place, so it's hard to watch, it's hard to understand, it's just hard all around. Noah always tried to smile for me. Even when he couldn't speak I knew how he felt because he had a little notepad he wrote on.

I stared down at the note he'd just written and rolled my eyes. "Get naked? Really?"

He just shrugged and scribbled a horrible picture of what looked like naked stick figures, one had a giant penis, and the other had breasts that fell past her waist.

"Drawing isn't your strong suit."

He scribbled something else down and showed it to me. The penis had grown, fantastic.

He made a choking noise that sounded like laughter, but when I looked up, he was actually choking, starting to turn blue.

I hit the call button, freaked out, only to get shoved out of the way when the nurse came running in.

"He just started choking!" I said, my cheeks stained with tears. "He wasn't even eating!"

"Anaphylaxis," the nurse stated as she grabbed something from a crash cart and inserted it into his IV. They said words I didn't understand and ran around his bed poking him, keeping him alive, and all I kept thinking was, It's okay to let go.

Because this wasn't living.

It wasn't.

We later found out that he had an allergic reaction to a new medication, and because his body was so tired of fighting, it reacted as if it was attacking his system.

Just one more drug he could no longer take.

That was the beginning of the end, that night.

We both lay awake staring at each other. He wasn't writing anything down, but he didn't need to. Instead, he was playing with my hair, rubbing my arm, making sure I knew that he was awake, that he was there.

And because I needed him to know it was okay, because I loved him, I asked him the hard question. "Noah, are you fighting because of me or because of you?"

He stilled.

"That's my answer, isn't it?" I looked up at him as he slowly nodded, tears filling his eyes. "You're tired, aren't you?"

A tear slid down his cheek. I buried my face in his chest, I inhaled his scent that was so uniquely him, citrusy and masculine all wrapped up into one. I squeezed his hand even though the squeeze back was so weak I wanted to weep.

"Okay," I whispered through my tears. "It's okay."

He shook his head violently. I didn't want him to have another attack, so I tried calming him down. He pointed at the pen and paper.

I quickly got it from the table and handed it to him. His writing was getting slower and slower but his penmanship was still incredible.

After a few minutes with shaking hands he handed me the paper. I read it out loud. "I don't want your last moments with me to be traumatic, I don't want to fall asleep and have you watch in horror when my eyes don't open. I can't handle knowing that the last moments you have with me are sad ones. But I don't know how to make it better. I don't want you to fucking remember this and cry. I want you to remember the burrito, the food fights we almost had every time we had a meal and I refused to share. I would die for you, Keaton—but I draw the line at dying in your arms."

My throat hurt from holding my tears in. "I get to decide what my last moments are with you, not you, Noah. I've given you everything, give me this one thing . . ." Hot tears burned my eyes then ran down my cheeks. "Let me hold your hand and walk you into heaven." A fat tear rolled down his cheek. "Please."

He grabbed the pen again and scribbled something down. He held up the paper to me, and in giant letters it said, "Okay."

I'll remember that moment forever. It was New Year's, people were singing and celebrating the fact that they had one more year, and I was holding his hand celebrating the fact that he'd been given all the years he would have, and that was okay. Snow started to fall outside, coating the ground in white. I squeezed his hand and kissed his knuckles. "I love you, Noah."

He brought our joined hands to his heart, keeping them pressed against his chest, then turned his head to watch the snow fall.

The last thing Noah saw on this earth was the cleansing beauty of snow, and the last thing I saw before the strength fully left his hand was a peaceful smile on his face. And the last sound he heard was the piercing cry of the woman he loved, shouting for anyone who would hear. "He's gone!"

She stopped talking while I watched the emotions war across her face. "I'm so sorry, Keaton."

She sniffled and wiped the tears away. "It was a beautiful ending."

"Some might even say perfect," I added, my stomach clenching, my heart breaking for this beautiful girl. "Do you want to call it quits for the day?"

"Maybe." She sniffled. "I don't know. We're so close to the end that—" She stopped talking as her eyes widened.

Curious as to what she was staring at, I followed her gaze outside.

It was snowing.

Snowing in the city.

When I looked back, Keaton was swaying a bit in her seat. I quickly moved to grab her, catching her right before she passed out in my arms.

Enough was enough.

She'd been puking.

And now she'd passed out.

Yes, it was emotionally heavy stuff, but she was freaking me the hell out. I called down to Barry. "Is the car downstairs?"

"Yes, sir."

"Good, I need it. We're headed to Manhattan Grace."

I just hoped everything was okay, and I mentally slapped myself for thinking she could handle all of this while not feeling well.

Keaton agreed to go once she came to a few seconds later. The ride to the hospital was strange. We'd just been talking about death, and now we were headed to the ER.

I hated every minute of it.

But something was wrong.

And even through her repeated mumbles that I was overreacting, I put my foot down. When we made it to the ER, we were promptly escorted to a private room, which I was thankful for. The last thing we needed was more bad press. I didn't care, but I did care about Keaton's health, and if that's what was affecting it, I knew what I needed to do.

Back the hell off.

She was more important than that.

"Hi." A doctor poked her head in the door. "My nurse said you've been vomiting and just passed out today? How long has this been going on?"

Keaton and I shared the same look of *Who knows?*

I spoke first. "A couple of days or so?"

"Any other symptoms?" The doctor looked concerned.

My stomach dropped. She was fine, she had to be fine.

"No." Keaton shook her head. "But I do think it's stress."

"Could be." The doctor nodded then smiled kindly. "Why don't we rule out the easy things first, like the flu, an infection, pregnancy . . ." As her voice trailed off, my eyes grew a bit too large for my head, meeting Keaton's.

She squinted down at her hands then up at me and looked ready to puke again. "Julian . . ."

The doctor glanced between us. "Something wrong?"

I don't know how I knew, just that I did. That would make sense, wouldn't it? It wasn't like we used protection the first time. Hell, I didn't even think about it. I don't think either of us were thinking about anything except for the pain to fucking stop.

It had to have been that first time.

I ran my hands through my hair. "I think she needs a pregnancy test."

Keaton's panicked expression wasn't helping the wild thumping of my heart as I grabbed her hand and waited for the doctor to come back.

Instead, it was a nurse who asked Keaton to pee in a cup, and what was only ten minutes ended up feeling like a thousand years as we waited in that room for them to tell us something that would alter us forever.

It was almost too much.

The snow falling outside.

Finishing the book.

Writing "The End."

And the possibility of a new life.

The nurse returned with a smile on her face. "Congratulations. It's early, looks like you're around three weeks, possibly four, though it's hard to tell. Your hCG is reading really high. Congrats again, you're going to be a mom!"

Keaton squeezed my hand so hard I was afraid it was going to fall off.

And then she burst into tears.

I quickly pulled her into my arms and held her. "Hey, hey, it's going to be okay."

"No." She sobbed harder against my chest. "Because people are going to know it's not his."

Had she stabbed me in the heart—it would have hurt less than those words. I pulled away and stared at her in disbelief. "Are you serious right now?"

She hiccupped out another sob. "Julian, dating is one thing! Having a baby is—everyone's going to know!"

"Then let them know!" I roared. "Why the hell do you care what they think?"

"Because I promised him!" she yelled right back. "I have a lucrative book deal based on my undying love for a man who died eleven months ago! What happens when they find out that I moved on and had a baby? Nobody's going to believe it was real. Nobody's going to care about him anymore!"

"It's not him you're worried about," I said with hurt in my voice. "It's you."

"What?" she hissed, her expression one of shock and irritation.

"This book . . . this isn't about him, Keaton. He's not here. This was only ever closure for you, and I'm sure he knew that, I'm sure he hoped it would help. But whether or not people believe your story has nothing to do with you writing it. He asked you to write it. He didn't ask people to believe it or even read it. You're the one doing that. You're the one existing in this in-between space where you can't let him go and we can't be together. You say you want that, but you want everything to be tied up in these neat little bows. That's not fucking life, trust me. I would know." I hung my head. "And the really sad part? You're making this about you when it's about us, when it affects both of us, when I can't think of anything that would make me happier than being a dad to a little girl who has clear blue eyes just like you, or a little boy with dirty hands he refuses to wash. And you're sitting there feeling sorry for yourself because of what people are going to say. I'm not trying to say your feelings aren't valid. I'm just saying mine are too, and unless you can write 'The End,' you can't move on, because you won't let yourself." I stopped talking, too upset to say anything more. "I'm going to go grab some coffee. Do you want juice? Water?"

"W-water." Her voice cracked.

I walked toward the door and paused, my hands anchored on the doorjamb as I allowed my head to fall forward. "I'm not leaving you," I said without looking back. "I just need space. I need time to think, and I don't want to hurt you any more than you want to hurt me, but that's what you keep doing, over and over again without realizing it, and I can take a lot, Keaton, I've lived with that sort of rejection my entire life, I can take one more. What I can't take is the fact that I'm falling in love with you—and that doesn't even seem to be a factor in your decisions."

I left and paced the hall. I knew that I could find something to drink close by, I'd visited this hospital often.

Izzy used to volunteer.

People used to whisper when I walked the halls.

They never really knew me, just through her, and to them I was this larger-than-life hero with a bad-boy streak and a roaming eye.

Now I just felt heartbroken.

A child.

She was pregnant with our child.

And the first words out of her mouth basically said she was sorry it was mine.

Damn it, I wished my mom was there.

I took a sip of the strong coffee and grabbed a bottle of water, then hung outside her room. I'd only been gone a few minutes, and I wasn't ready to go back in, I wasn't ready to see the look on her face.

Feel the disappointment thick in the air.

I grabbed my phone and dialed a familiar number.

My own voice mail.

I pressed play on the one I'd saved.

"Julian!" Mom's voice was filled with laughter. "Did you drop off all those historical romance novels? They aren't even out yet! Who did you sell your soul to? I won't care, I just want to sell mine too. These are my favorite authors! Have I ever told you how proud I am of you? Or how much I love you? And not just because you bought me books, though that doesn't hurt. I know you're still upset with your brother and I know I keep beating a dead horse, but . . . I just want to know that my boys have found love and forgiveness with each other. It's all we have on this earth, Julian. Money is fleeting, you know this, but love, love is forever, and Bridge loves you—so does Izzy. I want you to know I keep asking every nurse if they're single, and I think most would leave their husbands for you. Hah-hah, that's horrible. Don't laugh, I'm the worst at joking." I smiled as tears slipped down my cheeks. "Okay, another doctor's going to poke me with something that's supposed to make it better when we all know it makes it feel worse. Never forget who you are, Julian—mine. My son. The best son in the world." The voice mail ended.

I stared straight ahead.

And then I did something I hadn't done in a long time.

I called my brother.

"Julian?"

"I'm at the hospital."

"Shit, are you okay? I'm on my way . . ." I could hear him tripping over things.

"No, Bridge, I'm fine. I'm not here because I'm injured. Keaton hadn't been feeling well. She passed out—she's pregnant." I just blurted it.

The line went silent and then, "Are you calling because you're excited or because you're in need of a few paper bags to breathe into and a scrip for Xanax?"

I actually smiled at that. "I'm excited. She's . . . struggling."

His sigh was heavy. "Let her come to terms with it. It's been a really hard year for you, for her, and honestly, man, the media hasn't been the kindest to her. I know you've been avoiding it, but the comments on her last Instagram post are enough to make you sick. On top of that, the girl from the restaurant sold the picture to some celebrity gossip blog. They put you guys on their front page. I didn't want to tell you, but there's speculation all over the place, and people still aren't over his death, over this love story between them, so they don't understand how *she* could be."

"It makes sense," I admitted. "It just . . . hurts."

"Love hurts," he said frankly. "It's not easy, and even though you don't want to talk about it, it's not like it was easy for me and Izzy. I mean pretending to be a dick all the time was completely exhausting."

"Fuck you." I laughed.

He joined in. "I betrayed her, remember? I accepted money because I thought it would help. I wasn't guilt-free, and then I took her, stole her, not realizing the full story. My point is this: you fight for love because the minute you have a taste of it, you realize why wars are fought in honor of it. It's the most precious thing in the world, and it's worth waiting for . . . and fighting for."

I licked my dry lips. "When did you get so smart?"

"I take pills, though I think they're for erections since they're blue?"

"You just had to make a joke." I snorted out a laugh.

"Hey, brother . . ."

"Yeah?"

"Good to have you back."

"What do you mean?"

"It's your laugh, the real laugh, not the one you use in public. It's the one that means you're actually happy despite the shit storm you're in—it's good to have you back."

"It's good to be back."

"Now go tell her you love her."

"On it." I was about to hang up when I stopped and said, "Thanks, brother."

"Any time."

I smiled and slid the phone into my pants, then went back into the room.

The very empty room.

I looked around. Maybe she was in the bathroom?

Panicked, I walked out and asked the nurse where she was, only to have the nurse give me a funny look. "She was just discharged."

"That fast?"

"We aren't that busy today." Her look intensified. "Are you okay?"

"Yeah." Just heartbroken, abandoned, pissed. "I'm fine."

I tossed my coffee in the trash and made my way out of the hospital as fresh stupid snow fell all over me.

And I cursed Noah to hell for making it impossible to love the person he left behind.

Ten minutes went by.

Another twenty.

I shouldn't be upset, because it was my fault. "I'm so sorry, Julian," I murmured.

"Me too," came his voice.

I jolted up out of bed. He looked like I felt.

Absolute hell.

I burst into tears when he made his way over to me and pulled me into his arms. "Did you mean it?"

"No! Of course not, I was just upset, I think I love you—no, I *know* I love you and this baby—" I stopped. "Why are you smiling at me?"

"I meant what you typed on the computer, did you mean it?"

I nodded, not trusting my voice. "Yes."

"You typed 'The End.'"

"Because I knew I needed to make room for a new beginning," I admitted. "One with you."

"Not just me." Julian grinned. "With us." He touched my stomach. Butterflies erupted as he stared at me in awe and said, "It's going to be a boy."

"Men!" I laughed through my tears.

"But even if it's a girl . . . we're going to call her—"

"Your mom's name, we're going to name her after your mom."

He sucked in a breath. While I watched him and wondered out loud, "What did I ever do to deserve you?"

"Easy." He kissed the tears streaking down my cheeks. "Snuck into my cabin with a pointy weapon and tried to fight an elk for my love."

"Um, that's not exactly how things—"

He kissed my words away. "So we remember things differently."

"You threatened me—" Another searing kiss, and then I forgot all about what I was going to say as he peeled my shirt over my head and made me forget every single protest I could have possibly had against arguing.

And when we were naked in our bed, a tangle of arms, legs, mouths, and confessions, I realized that even if it's messy and makes no sense—that doesn't mean your love is any less real or true.

It just means it's different.

"My heart grew for you too," Julian whispered against my lips. "Now about that cat . . ."

Epilogue

JULIAN

The cabin
Three years later

"YOU DID NOT JUST BUILD A FORT WITHOUT ME!" Bridge shouted over the mountain of snow Izzy had built to barricade herself in. Their little Jill looked like she belonged in *A Christmas Story* as she tried to meander from the snowball stash back behind the fort for protection, and Leila, well, Leila was just making snow angels then stomping in them for the sheer joy of making snow go everywhere.

I shared a look with Keaton, who had just picked Leila up and was nuzzling her cold face when another snowball came flying by my ear. "Bridge, I will end you!"

"You will end me?" he mocked. "Could you sound any more like a dad right now?"

I burst out laughing and then ducked as another snowball came flying. He really did have great aim.

Had someone told me a few years back that I'd be back at my family's cabin with my own family, with my brother, his wife, my wife . . . our kids, I would have scowled and laughed in disbelief.

Now, it was everything.

My family was everything.

My wife.

My child.

Our future children.

I'd like to say that the minute the story was published, things were perfect. They weren't. We realized very soon how much privacy we would need for our family, to protect ourselves from people who had no business judging the way we lived our lives.

People were angry at first that she moved on. Angry that I helped her write the story, and the angriest are usually the loudest. The book spent weeks on all the bestseller lists, and slowly but surely people started to see we were real, that our love wasn't just something born out of loneliness or publicity, but something real. It helped that we did almost all of the press tour for her book together, holding hands, explaining how we fell in love, much to the joy of every single person who interviewed us and was moved to tears by the time the interview was done.

The response after our little girl was born was more gentle, maybe because people saw that what we had wasn't a fling, or maybe they just sensed our love for each other wasn't fleeting but forever.

I proposed when she was six months pregnant, and married her when Leila was old enough to attempt to be the best ring bearer in the city.

And I let go of the guilt.

It didn't happen fast.

It was a slow unpacking of years' worth of guilt for not being there for my mom, for caring more about my dad, and it was becoming a dad myself that helped me realize that fathers are still human, still struggling to do the best we can in a world that doesn't make it easy.

And I found out that Keaton was right. Love grows; it grows until it can't be contained, and then it grows some more.

Another snowball went flying. I sent Keaton a helpless look. "Are you going to watch me protect Winterfell all by myself?"

She rolled her eyes. "You and that show . . ."

"HEY!" Bridge stood like he was offended.

Bingo.

Direct hit as my snowball sailed into his face, covering him in snow. "Hey, you okay, man?"

"That's it." He started charging toward me, only to slip on more snow and get it in his pants. More shouting, cursing as both moms covered tender, young ears. And rather than feel guilty that I was missing out, I was thankful for the time I had now.

To not just make things right with my brother.

But to make my mom truly proud, by being a good father.

Acknowledgments

As always, I'm so thankful to God that I can write stories and that I get to work with amazing publishers like Skyscape, who truly want to bring that story to life, and to every single ravenous reader out there! My husband was super helpful with this book. I kept telling him I had this story idea, and he was the one that was like, "Well, write it!" I could not have done it without the help of Maria, my amazing editor who basically went, "You can do better, lol." Hey, sometimes we need tough love like that! I don't think I've ever been stretched so much (in a good way). This story and the one it follows are a part of my soul, and I felt like they needed to be told. Thank you to my insanely awesome beta readers, who helped me every step of the way even when I had to do a slight rewrite. To Melody and Kay, my editors, who helped pick out the places where I could make the book stronger. And to all of the Rockin' Readers who put up with me constantly teasing them with excerpts! Nina, Jill, Becca, Erica, you've all helped so much, especially with my writing schedule and helping me navigate what has easily been the most stressful, heartbreaking, yet incredible year of my life. To the bloggers and readers who support us authors constantly, I really won't ever be able to thank you enough. You are the reason I get to do what

I love, I am eternally grateful for your support and loyalty, and I hope you enjoyed this one! If you want to catch up, you can find me on www. rachelvandykenauthor.com or on Insta/Twitter @RacheVD. If you're feeling frisky, join my interactive reader group via Facebook: Rachel's New Rockin' Readers! Until next time! Hugs, RVD.

About the Author

Photo © 2014 Lauren Watson Perry, Perrywinkle Photography

Rachel Van Dyken is a *Wall Street Journal*, *USA Today*, and number-one *New York Times* bestselling author of Regency, paranormal, and contemporary romances. Her books include *Stealing Her* in the Covet series; the Red Card novels, *Risky Play* and *Kickin' It*; her Liars, Inc., series; and her Wingmen Inc. series, which has been optioned for film. A fan of *The Bachelor*, Starbucks coffee, and Swedish Fish (not necessarily in that order), Rachel lives in Idaho with her husband and her adorable son. For more information about Rachel's books and events, visit www. RachelVanDykenauthor.com.